BULL IN A TEA SHOP

BODYGUARD SHIFTERS #5

ZOE CHANT

Bull in a Tea Shop

Author's Note

This book stands alone and contains a complete HEA romance. However, if you'd like to read the other books in the Bodyguard Shifters series, here's the series so far, in order:

1. Bearista (Derek & Gaby's book)
2. Pet Rescue Panther (Ben & Tessa's book)
3. Bear in a Bookshop (Gunnar & Melody's book)
4. Day Care Dragon (Darius & Loretta's book)
5. Bull in a Tea Shop (Maddox & Verity's book)
6. Dancer Dragon (Heikon & Esme's book)
7. Babysitter Bear (Dan & Paula's book)

And don't miss the spinoff series, Stone Shifters:
1. Stoneskin Dragon (Reive & Jess's book)
2. Stonewing Guardian (Mace & Thea's book)

You may also enjoy Bodyguard Shifters Collection 1, collecting books 1-4.

MADDOX

The truck pulled over to let Maddox off on the wide gravel shoulder of the highway, next to a painted wooden sign in a field of goldenrod and thistles. In old-timey letters the sign announced: SILVERMINE, ARIZONA, POP. 1643. And below that: "A Friendly Place To Live."

Yeah, maybe, Maddox thought with a slight smile, *but not for people like me.*

"This look good to you, buddy?" the truck driver asked him.

"Looks just fine." Maddox collected his backpack, and reached down to retrieve the cane leaning against the seat by his leg. "Thanks, man. Buy you a burger as a thanks for the ride, if you want to stop for a while." It'd just about tap him out—he was down to his last few bucks. But hell, he had a blanket in the pack, and it wouldn't be the first time he'd slept in a field.

The trucker shook his head. "Nah, I want to get on into Flagstaff before dark. If you're looking for chow, there's a

1

pretty good diner in this town, though. It's called the Whistlestop."

"Thanks," Maddox said. He stepped down carefully to the gravel, taking a minute to find his balance on his stiffened-up leg and hip.

"Good luck, buddy," the trucker called down. "Hope you find what you're looking for."

Maddox grunted acknowledgement. The truck pulled out in a cloud of dust.

He looked after it for a minute, then shouldered the backpack and began limping along the side of the road that turned off the highway. He loathed the cane, but he had resigned himself to the fact that he couldn't walk very far without it, at least not without being in excruciating pain afterwards.

It had been a year since he'd hurt his leg, in a past he didn't talk about, at least not to the kind of people that he tended to meet in mom-and-pop cafés in small towns along the highway. Mostly, he tried not to think about it much.

Hope you find what you're looking for ... yeah, that would be hard, since he didn't even know what that was. He just knew that the life he'd left behind wasn't it.

He kept moving because it made it easier not to look back.

But it was a pretty place here. Damn, it was pretty. He hadn't been in the Southwest much, and he drank in the clear, dry air and the sharp beauty of the mountains against vivid sunset skies. The higher slopes were dusted with gold as the aspens and cottonwoods turned colors; farther down, the hills were tawny as a lion's flanks.

Maddox thought he might like to find out what winter in the desert was like. It wasn't as if he had anywhere else to be.

He could see the town across the open countryside, roofs of buildings and radio or cell towers and a water tower, but it looked like the road wound around in a big loop before it got there, following some old right-of-way. No reason why he had to go the long way, though. Maddox ducked under some strands of wire cattle fencing and began to walk across the pasture as the sky went from pink to purple overhead.

It took him a few steps to get his equilibrium on the rougher ground of the pasture; his bad leg kept trying to throw him off. But once he got the hang of it, it was easier than walking on the road's soft shoulder. There were a few cows here, settling down for the night. The herd's bull grunted at him. Maddox grunted back, and the bull gave him a long stare before deciding he posed no threat to the cows and settling down again.

Maddox felt his bull stir slightly inside him, before it sank back into the depths of his soul. He hadn't been in touch with his bull much since his injury, and what little contact they'd had was strained. He wondered if such a huge and powerful beast as it had once been was ashamed of what Maddox had allowed them both to become.

Once, he'd made his living with his muscles. As a bull or as a man, Maddox was huge and intimidating, afraid of no one. He was still a big man, still in good shape, but a man who walked with a limp and a cane couldn't intimidate people as a bouncer or bodyguard. He couldn't even get physical labor in a warehouse or on a farm, though he would have appreciated a job like that, some kind of thing where he could lose himself in the physical activity and forget about everything else for a while.

Walking was that way, a little. It cleared his head. And his senses were still shifter-sharp. On the evening air, a sudden sound broke through the quiet and peace of the countryside: the sound of someone distantly screaming. It sounded like a woman's voice.

Startled, Maddox turned and picked up his pace, plunging

through thorny brush and clambering with difficulty across rocky ground.

He came to the top of a small ridge in the purpling dusk. Below him, the headlights of a couple of vehicles—one with sheriff's markings, the other a massive brand-new truck—illuminated a small cluster of people.

Two of them were teenagers, Maddox saw in surprise. Just kids, a girl and a boy. It was the girl who was screaming. A big, muscular man was holding her. Another had the boy in an armlock. There were a couple more thug types in front of them, along with a man in a sheriff's uniform.

"Let him go!" the girl cried. She tried to kick the man holding her. Looking at the rage twisting her face, Maddox thought her earlier screams had been fury more than fear. She had a short, spiky hairdo and jeans ripped in the intentional way that some people liked. The boy had a long pony-tail and dark, hawkish features.

"Now, Bailey," the sheriff said. "We can't have you two messing around in our business, can we?"

He turned his head, and that was the point when Maddox noticed another man standing at the edge of the circle of headlights, quietly watching the proceedings. Everything about him screamed "money." He wore a nice suit and his graying hair was slicked back. He couldn't have looked more out of place in this cow pasture.

But Maddox would lay odds that this was the guy calling the shots, and he knew it for sure when Gray Hair gave a small nod to the sheriff.

"Teach him a lesson," the sheriff said.

One of the thugs drove a fist into the boy's stomach, and at that point Maddox had had enough.

"Hey!" he bellowed down the hill. "Let 'em alone."

He had their attention, certainly. As he limped down the

hill, he could see them take in first his huge size, and then the cane and the limp.

"Son," the sheriff said, "this doesn't concern you. Just keep walking."

"I'm not your son," Maddox said. "Let these kids go. Pick on someone your own size."

The gray-haired man spoke up in a smooth, cultured voice. "You're messing with something you don't understand. These 'kids,' as you call them, are a public nuisance to the good businesspeople of this town."

"I don't care," Maddox said flatly. "If they broke a law, arrest 'em. But that's not what you're doing, is it?" He glanced over the thugs. "I've been where you guys are. This was my job too, once. I'm gonna say this one more time: let these kids go, or you're gonna have a problem."

The sheriff laughed. "We're not gonna hurt 'em. Just scare 'em some."

"You don't have to explain yourself to him," Gray Hair said calmly. "Walk away, boy. Or else *you're* the one who's going to have a problem."

Maddox could see the way they'd taken in his cane and limp, and then dismissed him as a threat. He sighed, measured the distance carefully between him and each of them—this kind of thing took more planning these days than it used to—and then moved.

A punch that had the strength of a bull behind it lifted the thug holding the girl off the ground and dropped him. The girl stumbled forward, free. Maddox was already turning around to slam his cane into the kneecaps of the one holding the boy.

The two young people scrambled away, clutching each other. The sheriff was reaching for his gun, but Maddox moved with shifter speed and punched him in the gut, the same way the sheriff had ordered his men to hit the boy. The sheriff doubled over with a gusty breath, and Maddox spun to punch the last standing thug, sending him to the ground.

It had taken no more than seconds.

Maddox glanced at Gray Hair to make sure the well-dressed ringleader wasn't going to try to interfere. Gray Hair just stared at him. So did the teenagers, wide-eyed and clinging to each other a few yards away.

"Go on," Maddox told them. "Get somewhere safe."

They didn't need to be told twice. As the two of them vanished into the darkness, Gray Hair said in a voice that was perfectly calm, "You've got some balls on you, son, I'll grant you that. Are you interested in a job?"

Maddox let out a short laugh. "I've spent too much of my life working for men like you."

"I'll make it worth your while. I could use a man with your talents."

"Didn't you just hear me say no?"

The way the guy was looking at him, it was clear that this old jerk wasn't used to people saying no to him. Maddox knew his type, all right. His last employer, Darius, had been like that in the beginning, though he'd changed toward the end. And before him, there had been a string of bad men like this one, making Maddox do things he now regretted down to the bottom of his soul.

He hadn't been able to do this to them, but this man was just as deserving.

Maddox punched him in the face.

Gray Hair didn't even try to dodge; he obviously didn't expect it. Maddox pulled his punch somewhat, not wanting to do serious damage, because it was clear that this guy—unlike the sheriff and his men—didn't know how to take a punch. Still, Gray Hair went down flat on his backside, getting his nice pants covered with dirt and cow pats.

He stared up at Maddox in shock, his composure shattered, clutching at his face and nose with blood welling up between his fingers.

"You *hit* me!" he said, muffled.

"You just ordered your thugs to beat up a couple of kids. I'd say you had it coming." Maddox turned his back on the man on the ground, on the groaning sheriff and his men, and limped off into the gathering night.

"You've made a mistake!" Gray Hair shouted after him. "You're going to regret this!"

Yeah, he already did, actually. As soon as the darkness had covered his retreat, Maddox switched from his unconcerned saunter to the fastest stride he could manage with his bad leg, just short of a run.

Yeah, that's it, piss off the guy who's probably the number one big shot around these parts. Good thing he wasn't planning on sticking around this town very long.

The sound of an engine roaring up behind him made Maddox duck off into the brush. The headlights raked across the road, and the big truck and sheriff's cruiser rocketed past him, spraying dirt and gravel from under their tires. Once they were gone, Maddox picked himself up and brushed himself off.

Yeah, he might ought to forget spending the night in this town. He thought about walking straight back to the highway and thumbing a ride, but he was hungry enough that he decided to grab a burger to go from the first place he found in town that had food and was open. And *then* he'd walk back to the highway and thumb a ride.

Sorry, kids. He hoped they had the sense to stay out of sight for a while.

He was no longer quite as worried by the time he got to the edge of town. It was full dark now, the last light vanishing from the sky over the mountains. Just ahead of him was an inviting little Main Street done up like an Old

West town, with colorful false fronts on the buildings and wrought-iron lampposts glowing warmly on the street-corners. It did look like a nice little place. A sign halfway down the street read WHISTLESTOP CAFÉ. He quickened his stride again, looking forward to getting some food and a hot cup of coffee. Maybe he'd just hang around the diner 'til the sheriff got tired of looking for him, then see if he could hitch a ride up to the highway ...

He was keeping an eye open for headlights, and one ear cocked for any vehicles coming up on him. But the sudden revving of an engine didn't ping him as a danger sound until it was too late. With no headlights, the dark bulk of a large vehicle came out of nowhere; it had been parked behind a billboard, lying in wait. It slammed into Maddox from behind, and sent him tumbling down the embankment into the ditch.

Despite the shock and pain, he wasn't completely knocked out. He lay dazed in the ditch, and heard the sound of a car door slamming over the rumbling of a large engine, and men's voices.

They're coming to finish you off, he told himself. *Do something. Get up!*

His bad leg was completely useless, and it felt like he'd done something to the ankle of the other leg as well. When he started to pick himself up, pain stabbed him viciously in the side. *Ribs*, he thought, panting through the agony. Cracked or broken. There was a splitting pain in his head and blood running into his eyes.

But none of that would matter if he couldn't get out of this ditch in the next few seconds without being seen.

Flashlights raked across the rocks above him. Breathing through his mouth, trying not to make noise, he used the cane as a support to struggle to his feet. One of the back-pack's straps had come loose, and he had to slip out of the other one; there was no way he could move stealthily while wearing it. There wasn't anything in it that he'd mind losing too much. Just some camping supplies, a change of clothes, and a couple of paperback books.

"Down there!" he heard someone say.

Nothing like being well motivated. The first few steps were agonizing, but he managed to stumble into the brush.

If only he could shift ... but after all these months of avoiding contact with his bull, when he reached down inside himself, it simply wasn't there. It was like there was a wall between him and his animal.

Come on, come on ... In the dark, it was hard to see where he was going. He just knew that he needed to get away from the road.

"Hey!" a voice whispered. "Hey, mister!"

Maddox flinched and managed to support himself unsteadily on both feet so he could swing the cane into a defensive position.

"It's us!"

The girl with the spiked punk hair emerged from the bushes. Her boyfriend was a step behind her.

"Come on," the boy whispered. "You're only in trouble because of us. We'll help hide you."

Maddox didn't think they were lying, and anyway, they were just kids, and human kids at that. If he was going to have to fight somebody in his current condition, he'd much rather go up against a couple of teenage punks than a bunch of armed thugs.

He let the kids lead him away from the road, deeper into the darkness. He wasn't sure how much longer he could keep going. His mouth tasted like blood, and deep pain stabbed his side at every breath. Only shifter resilience kept him on his feet.

A small hand touched his arm cautiously. He jerked away.

"Sorry!" the girl said. "You can, uh, lean on me? If you need it. You're breathing really loud."

He didn't take her up on the offer, but he tried to breathe quieter. It was really dark here. The kids were leading him through a band of trees behind some houses. He could still see flashlights in the woods behind him.

"Where should we take him?" the boy whispered. "He needs help. We can't just leave him behind a bush or something."

"Aunt Verity's place," the girl said after a moment.

"Your aunt's gonna kill you."

"I know, but where else can we go? When we explain how he helped us, she won't mind, I hope."

"Yeah, but that'll mean telling her what we did this afternoon, and then she's going to kill you even *more*."

"What'd you do?" Maddox asked. His voice came out thick and hoarse.

"Uh ..." the boy said.

"Classified," the girl said quickly.

Maddox's knees tried to buckle before he could ask more questions, and pain washed everything else out of his head. Hands touched him again, one of the kids supporting him on each side, and this time he was unable to fend off their help.

"You'll be okay," the girl whispered. "We're almost to my aunt's place."

"She's gonna *kill* you."

"Shut up, Luke! If you want to leave, you can leave."

There was no answer from Luke, but he didn't move away. Maddox clenched his teeth and pushed them off him, one at a time. "I can walk by myself," he gritted out.

They moved back, but continued to hover, looking up at him with wide eyes like anxious little deer.

"Here we are," the girl said suddenly, and unlatched a gate

in a wooden fence. They entered some kind of garden. Maddox smelled fragrant flowers.

What kind of place had they taken him to? The garden was a dark blur, but looking up, he glimpsed a pretty little two-story house, an old-fashioned kind of house with a pointy roof and dormer windows.

It *looked* like the sort of place that would be owned by someone's aunt. In a small town like this, the aunt probably owned an antique store and had doilies on everything. And she definitely wasn't going to appreciate a guest who was covered in dirt and blood, and had a bunch of thugs after him.

"You can't take me in there," he whispered, pulling back.

The girl planted her feet and tried to tug him onward. "It's my aunt Verity's place. She's blind. She won't even know you're there. I'll just sneak you up the back stairs—"

"Are you kidding? Your aunt has ears like a bat," Luke whispered.

Worse and worse. The last thing he wanted was to get some poor elderly blind woman involved. "Look, is there a garden shed or something? I can hide there until they stop looking."

"We can't just put you in the *shed*!"

"Your aunt's going to hear us out here," Luke whispered.

That seemed to help her make a decision, and the two of them led Maddox through a bunch of strong-smelling plants to a pretty little garden shed that looked more like a doll-house, what little of it he could see in the moonlight. The girl opened the door. The interior was very dark and smelled like potting soil and compost. Maddox stumbled into a row of rakes and other tools, and caught himself on the edge of the door, panting through a rush of blinding pain.

"Are ... are you sure you're gonna be okay?" Luke whispered.

"Yeah, sure," Maddox said. He wasn't at all sure, but he thought he'd feel better if he could sit down.

"I'll go get some things from the house," the girl whispered. "Bandages and things."

"You don't have to—" Maddox began, but they'd already hurried off into the garden, leaving him alone in the shed.

He found a pile of bags of compost to sit on, and leaned painfully back against the wall, closing his eyes.

This wasn't the best night he'd ever had, for sure.

VERITY

V erity Breslin was humming quietly to herself and going through the nightly ritual of closing up the tea shop when there was a commotion in the back yard.

She was alone in the shop. Her niece Bailey worked part time at the store after school as well as living with Verity in their shared apartment above the shop, but Bailey had called earlier to ask if she could take the afternoon off for some kind of after-school activity with her boyfriend and his friends. Verity hadn't been too clear on the details, but Bailey was a good girl despite the punk attitude she liked to cultivate, and she'd been working hard lately. She deserved some time off. Although Bailey had lived with her for several years now, Verity still struggled with the tightrope act that parenting a teenager required. She didn't want to be too strict and deprive Bailey of some well-deserved freedom.

Anyway, it wasn't as if she'd expected the store to be busy this afternoon, and she hadn't been wrong. Ducker's harassment campaign had been terrible for business. She'd had just one customer all day, old Mrs. Yazzie who had come into town on her monthly trip from the sheep ranch she ran with her husband and son-in-law, picking up the usual bundles of herbs for the home remedies she made for her arthritis and her husband's gout. The herbs were already neatly packaged under the counter, and Verity found them by touch, running her fingers over the little paper Braille tag tied to the package and then checking with a quick sniff.

"Heard a rumor you were selling out and leaving," Mrs. Yazzie had said casually as Verity wrapped up her purchases.

"No," Verity replied firmly. "I'm not even considering it."

"See you got the front window replaced."

"Yes, ma'am, we did." The last time Mrs. Yazzie had been in the store, their front window had just recently had a brick thrown through it. Verity had dutifully gone through the motions of reporting it to Sheriff Hawkins, all the while knowing the sheriff had probably dispatched someone to throw the brick in the first place, or maybe even thrown it himself.

"Shame about those vandals," Mrs. Yazzie said, her voice all too sharp and knowing. "The Millers' antique store is closed now, looks like."

"They were thinking about retiring to a milder climate anyway," Verity said.

"Mmmm," was all Mrs. Yazzie said, and she claimed her packages and shuffled out.

Verity turned on her audiobook again and went back to mixing dried leaves for sachets of tea, sniffing occasionally to be sure she had the right flavors. She loved inventing new teas. Some were designed for specific purposes, to ease menstrual trouble or soothe digestive problems or calm the mind for sleeping. Others just tasted good.

She'd been running the tea shop for her entire adult life. Back in those early days, there were people in town who didn't believe a blind woman could run her own business.

14

She'd showed *them*, and after all her struggles starting up the shop, she wasn't about to sell out just because that fool Ducker and his pet sheriff thought they could strong-arm her out of business. Where would she go? What would she do? She couldn't imagine herself starting over somewhere new, where she didn't know anyone.

No, she was staying right here. They could throw rocks through her windows, harass her on the street, and make insulting offers to buy the building, but this was *hers*. Thank heaven she'd paid off the mortgage, because she could easily see Ducker strong-arming the bank into foreclosing. But there was nothing he could legally do to make her sell.

No ... all he could do was chase off her customers and threaten her.

And all of these thoughts were uppermost in her mind when there was a clattering in the backyard as she was going through her nightly ritual for closing up the shop. Her heart accelerated, but she calmly locked the cash drawer and then reached under the counter for the wrought-iron fireplace poker she'd started keeping there after the incident with the brick.

With the poker in one hand, and her other hand holding the cane she used to feel out her path when she went for walks outside, she listened at the back door. She heard whispered voices, and ... yes, footsteps on the back stairs that went up to the apartment above the shop.

Verity unlocked the door and stuck her head out. "Bailey!" she said sharply.

There was a guilty hush and the footsteps stopped. "Aunt Verity!" the girl's voice said. "I, uh. I can explain!"

"Is that boyfriend of yours with you?"

"Hi, Ms. Breslin," Luke's voice said guiltily.

"Bailey, are you really trying to sneak a boy up to your room? What is wrong with you?"

"We just didn't want to bother you," Bailey said. "I ... uh ... Luke left something in my room, and we had to get it, and now we're going out again. So everything is fine."

"Everything is certainly *not* fine." Verity stepped out onto the back porch and tilted her face up. In addition to the usual nighttime fragrances of her herb garden, she smelled something else. Something sharp. "Bailey, what do you have there?"

"Nothing?" Bailey said.

"I told you she has ears like a bat," Luke whispered. "And a nose like a bloodhound."

"The only difference between me and most people is that I pay attention to what's around me, that's all," Verity said sharply. "Come down here, you two."

Their footsteps shuffled nervously down the stairs. Something sloshed, and she finally figured out what the smell was.

"Bailey, what do you have the iodine for?"

"Um ... Luke cut himself!" Bailey blurted out. "On a ... on a fence. An old barbed wire fence. We were just doctoring it. Upstairs."

"I hope he's had his tetanus shots," Verity said. "That can be dangerous. Are you up to date on your shots, Luke?"

"Yes, ma'am," Luke said.

There was still something wrong. They seemed very guilty and subdued. And there was no reason why they'd be carrying the entire bottle of iodine if all they wanted to do was go upstairs to do first aid on some scrapes.

"What else do you have there, Bailey?"

"Nothing?" Bailey said, and just then there was a loud clatter and thump from somewhere in the garden.

Verity whirled around, raising the poker.

"Raccoons!" Bailey said. "I just—I just saw one!"

There was another clatter. "That's not raccoons," Verity

16

said quietly. "It sounds like someone's at the shed. Both of you, get into the house."

"Aunt Ver," Bailey said, her voice anxious. "There's something I need to tell you ..."

Verity had already begun to stalk down the path. She abandoned the cane against a garden bench so she had both hands for the poker. She had built every part of this garden, and she knew it so well that she could walk it as swiftly as any sighted person.

And she hated to think what one of Ducker's men might be doing in her backyard. Stealing something? Her blood ran cold at the idea of those bullies poking around in her things.

"Aunt Verity!" Bailey's voice said right behind her.

"I told you kids to go into the house!" Raising her voice, she called, "Whoever you are, you're trespassing on private property. Get off my land or I'll make you sorry."

A final small clatter from the shed seemed almost like an afterthought, as if whatever was making the noise was now holding very still, but one final trowel or flowerpot had been on the verge of teetering until it fell over.

"That's your final warning, then," Verity snapped, marching forward with the poker cocked up over her shoulder like a baseball bat—telling herself, at the same time, that she wasn't about to make a terrible mistake. They did get animals in town sometimes, even big ones, black bears and cougars coming down from the mountains. No one had been attacked by a wild animal in town for a long time, but there were incidents out on the rural roads and hiking trails; just last year a hiker's dog had been injured by coyotes, and livestock losses to wild animals weren't uncommon.

But she didn't think this was an animal. There was something about that flurry of activity, followed by a very purposeful hush, that made Verity think there had to be a human mind involved. Possibly a marginal example of the species, considering they'd broken into her garden and were now hiding in or behind her garden shed. She might even be insulted that Ducker wasn't wasting money on competent vandals to harass her.

"Come out of there!"

There were little rustles, a clink or two, and some anxious scuffling from the kids behind her. Then a voice—a deep, rumbling voice, a male voice—said very softly, "I didn't mean to scare you, ma'am."

Verity nearly dropped her poker.

"Aunt Verity," Bailey began in a small voice.

"Hush," Verity said sharply. "I'm sure whoever this is can speak for himself. Can't he?"

"Yes, ma'am," the deep, quiet voice said after a moment.

There was something about that voice's deep timbre that shivered in her bones. It was a voice that she wanted to lean into, a voice she yearned to hear again as soon as he stopped talking.

Verity had been blind from birth, so she had never learned to visualize things the way she understood other people did. She saw things in her own way, as a mix of impressions and feelings, touch and smell and a sort of general all-over sense of the shape of a thing.

And she desperately wanted to know what a man with a voice like that "looked" like. She could feel it already—the way his muscles would flex under her hands, the rasp of his stubble against her skin. She wanted to know what he smelled like, what he tasted like ...

But more than that, she wanted to know what he was doing in her garden shed.

MADDOX

M addox had been thinking he'd just slip away while the kids were in the house. He appreciated them helping him, but he didn't want to get this nice family in trouble.

He just hadn't figured on how hard it was going to be to get up once he sat down.

After stumbling into racks of garden tools and getting the whole household roused, he ended up sitting heavily on a pile of bags of what was probably manure from the smell, and that was where the angel with the fireplace poker found him.

He couldn't see much of her, between the darkness in the garden and the way his vision kept blurring in and out of focus. With the lights of the house gleaming behind her, all he could see was that she wore a long skirt swishing around her legs and wore her hair in two braids falling over the shoulders of her loose blouse. It was a girlish hairstyle, but he didn't think she was young. There was a solidity to her and a firm confidence in her low, rich voice that spoke of maturity.

He wished he could see her face, even enough to read her

expression. Most of all, he didn't want to scare her. Maddox knew he was intimidating even normally, with the tattoos and piercings and his massive size, and right now he was covered in dirt and blood and bruises.

So he stayed sitting down and hoped she hadn't already called the police.

But she didn't seem afraid. She came another step closer, a cautious step, but the kind of caution that he thought was more related to feeling her footing on the dark path than because she was afraid of him specifically.

"Why are you in my shed?" she demanded.

It was a fair question. He was still trying to figure out how to answer it in a way that wouldn't immediately cause her to run screaming for the house and call the cops when the punk girl made a throat-clearing noise and said, "Luke and I told him he could, Aunt Verity."

"What?" The poker-wielding angel—*Verity*, he thought; *her name is Verity*—rounded on the young couple, who both took a few hasty steps back. "Bailey Breslin, my garden shed is not a rest stop for vagrants! Is this a friend of yours?"

"No, he helped us and he's in trouble, Aunt Ver, just listen! The sheriff is after him."

"And you're hiding him *here*?"

"He helped us," Bailey declared, crossing her arms, while her boyfriend stared nervously at the poker. "He saved our lives. It's a long story, but we couldn't just leave him. He got hurt because of us."

"He's hurt?" Verity turned her head, not exactly looking at Maddox but cocking her head to the side as if she was listening instead. "How badly?"

"Not bad," Maddox said quickly, as Bailey said, "Pretty bad."

"You should take him to the clinic, then."

"No, Aunt Ver, you don't understand. Mr. Ducker and the

sheriff are after him. I mean, they're literally hunting him. They tried to kill him. If we took him there, they'd find him right away. And he helped us, when he didn't have to. We can't just hand him over to them."

"I'm going to want to hear this story," Verity muttered. She lowered the poker to her side, and turned back toward Maddox, with that same odd listening posture, not quite looking at him. *Is she really that afraid of me?* he thought. "So those first-aid things are for him, I assume."

"Um ..." The girl started to hold up her hands, which were full of gauze packets and other items Maddox couldn't see clearly, and then lowered them. "How did you know I—"

"Because I'm not *stupid*," Verity said tartly. "You, there. In the shed. How badly *are* you hurt?"

Maddox hesitated. "Not so bad I need to put you to any trouble," he said, finally.

Verity huffed out a sigh. "I haven't raised a teenager without knowing what *that* means," she said. "Come on. Why don't you come into the house and we'll see what we can do for you."

Maddox made a ferocious effort, leaning on the cane. The world tilted and red sparks wheeled in his vision; he could feel his ribs grinding together. He sank back onto the pile of manure sacks. "I ... don't think I can."

"You can't get up?!"

"No, ma'am," Maddox said quietly. He just hoped he could get through this conversation without passing out.

"This man should be in a hospital," Verity murmured. "Hold this." She thrust the poker in the general direction of the punk girl, who looked flustered and then shoved her first-aid supplies at her boyfriend and took it.

Then Verity stepped carefully in Maddox's direction, reached out with a light dancing touch of her fingers and swept her hand past the support for the shed roof, then rested her fingertips on it and held out her other hand, sort of in his general direction but not quite.

Maddox looked at it, and at her.

"Are you still awake? Still there?" Verity said. "I'm holding out my hand."

"I ... know," he said cautiously. "Do you want me to—"

"I'm blind. I can't see you. Take my hand so I know where you are."

"Oh," he said, startled. He had thought she was just trying very hard not to make eye contact with him. Suddenly a lot of things made more sense. This was the blind aunt, of course. He'd been expecting someone old.

He reached out and stopped with his hand just on the verge of taking hers. He didn't touch people very often. When he closed his fingers around her much smaller ones, the sensation was unexpectedly powerful. He was aware of the strength in her small fingers, the slight calluses from garden work or other physical labor, the softness of her palm.

He thought she was going to try to pull him up, but instead she moved forward, with a swiftness and assurance he wasn't expecting. She kept hold of his hand but before he knew it, her other arm had slipped around his back and slid beneath his arm to support him, and suddenly he had an armful of curvy woman.

Maddox tensed, which hurt a lot, but he was afraid to breathe, afraid to move. Her hair smelled like flowers.

"Are you just going to sit there?" Her words were impatient, but her voice was gentle. "Let's get you up."

He gasped aloud in pain as Verity heaved her weight against him to try to get him on his feet. She'd compressed his injured ribs, and for a minute his vision went white.

"Sorry," she said quickly, adjusting her grip. "Do you think you can handle stairs? My apartment is above the shop, and there's no elevator."

"I don't know," he admitted, still short of breath.

"We'll put you in the shop, then," she decided. "Luke, go open the door. Bailey, go upstairs and get some blankets."

With Verity helping and his cane to lean on, he managed to get painfully to his feet. The journey to the house was a slow hobble, and he couldn't help being acutely aware of her body against him: her warmth and softness, the strength of the arm around him, every whisper of her skirt and the soft brush of her braids when she moved her head.

"I'm Verity Breslin," she said. "What's your name?"

"Maddox." It came out on a grunt of pain.

"Is that first or last?"

"Murphy. Maddox Murphy." He'd simply gone by Maddox for so long that it sounded strange to hear his full name spoken aloud.

"Irish, is it?"

"Irish and Welsh. My family, not me."

"And what are you doing in our town, Maddox? I don't think you're from around here."

"No, ma'am," he said. The conversation gave him something to focus on other than his pain, which he thought was probably her intent. "I travel around. I'm just hitchhiking through. I stopped and ..."

He paused because he wasn't sure how much he should tell her of what had happened with the kids.

"You got in some kind of trouble," Verity said. "I figured out that much."

"It wasn't his fault," Bailey called out as she clattered down the stairs with a bowl of water; it was an external flight of stairs with a white-painted wooden railing leading up to the second floor. "He saved me and Luke from Sheriff Hawkins and Mr. Ducker's guys."

"And why did you need saving, exactly?" Verity's voice turned tart again. "When I told you that you could have the afternoon to spend with Luke, getting in trouble with the law wasn't what I meant. Did he try to *arrest* you?"

"He did more than that," Maddox said, grimacing as he made his way carefully onto the back patio. The back door stood open, with the boy, Luke, nervously hovering within. "When I found them, the sheriff and some of his men were beating up Luke here."

"*What?*" Verity said. "Don't tell me *you* need a hospital too!"

"They only hit me a couple of times," Luke mumbled. "Mr., uh, Maddox here stopped them."

"I will definitely need to hear this story," Verity said, "but first I need a full accounting of everyone's injuries, if people would be so kind as to tell me the truth this time. Bailey, take the cushions off the couch and spread the blanket over them, please."

A wave of nose-tingling smells hit Maddox with almost physical force as Verity helped him through the back door. Immediately he stumbled into a rack of jars, reeled away from that as Verity tried to steady him, and knocked his elbow into something that clinked and slid off its shelf. Maddox dropped his cane to grab a teapot shaped like an elephant and hastily put it back on its shelf. The cane teetered and started to fall into a brass tree holding a bunch of teacups. Bailey lunged forward and caught it, and for a minute everyone just stood there, afraid to move.

Then Verity said calmly, "Let's take this one step at a time, shall we? Bailey, do you have a place ready for me to put him?"

"Working on it, Aunt Verity." Bailey's voice was meek. She slid the head of the cane underneath Maddox's dangling hand and darted off.

24

Verity carefully maneuvered him through crowded shelves of jars and packets and bins, to a little coffee-shop corner area with padded furniture and colorful Southwest prints on the wall. As instructed, Bailey had laid out the couch cushions and draped a brightly patterned blanket over them. Verity found it with her foot and helped Maddox sit down on it.

"I'll need water, please," she said.

"Here, Aunt Ver." Bailey placed a damp cloth in her aunt's hand.

"Luke, could you go make sure the front door of the shop is locked and the closed sign is out? Now," Verity said, smiling, "I might need a little guidance here."

"Okay," Maddox managed faintly.

In the better light, he could finally get a good look at her. Her face was gorgeously unique, with a strong jaw and a nose with a bump in the middle, freckles heavily dusting both cheeks, a wide expressive mouth and equally expressive, heavy brows. Gray threaded through her thick brown braids, and her eyes were a clear darker gray that never quite locked gazes with his own.

Bailey hovered, passed items to her aunt, and quietly gave directions ("A little to the left; no, there's some dirt embedded there, you need to get it cleaner") as Verity cleaned up his cuts and scrapes with the wet cloth and iodine. This was clearly something they'd done before, because they were perfectly in sync, with Bailey anticipating Verity's need for clean gauze and fresh water, and Verity needing only slight verbal nudges to know exactly what her niece did. Maddox wondered if perhaps the usual patient was Bailey herself, providing sighted assistance as her aunt doctored her own childhood injuries.

But mostly he was enthralled by Verity herself, the soft curve of her cheek and downward cast of her dark lashes as she worked on his injuries. She didn't look like any TV blind person he'd ever seen. He had never known anyone in real life who was blind, and the way Verity looked at things, and especially at people, was nothing at all like the vacant, unfocused gaze of blind people on TV. It must just be a way of making seeing actors look blind for the TV audience, Maddox thought, because there was nothing at all vacant about Verity's sharp gray gaze. Her eyes weren't unfocused, but instead seemed to be looking with direction and intent toward something only she could see. When she spoke to someone, she turned and looked toward their face, so that Maddox had to keep reminding himself that she couldn't actually see anyone.

It felt a little weird watching her when she couldn't see him, but he couldn't seem to take his eyes off her. He'd never been this enraptured by anyone before. Even her tiniest movement captivated him, the way she pursed her lips as she focused on taping down a gauze bandage, the flutter of her lashes when she blinked—

"Sorry?" he said, realizing she'd said something to him this time and not to Bailey.

"I'm going to need you to take your shirt off."

"Oh." He wasn't normally shy about his body; shifters typically weren't. But he could feel his cheeks heating at the thought of—

... of what, though? She couldn't see him.

And yet he was oddly disappointed at that.

What's wrong with us? he queried his bull. *Is she our mate?* He'd always thought you'd just *know*. Everyone said it was supposed to be that way, that you'd look into another person's eyes and something would happen and you'd know you were meant to be with them forever. He hadn't felt anything like that, and yet right now he felt as if he could happily spend all of eternity just tracing Verity's freckles with his eyes.

I don't know, his bull replied unhelpfully.

Maybe the blow to the head had knocked him silly.

He struggled with his shirt, and in the end, Verity had to help him get it and then his ragged T-shirt off. Bailey turned very pink and averted her eyes as she went to get a clean bowl of water. When she came back, her teenage embarrassment turned to shock. "*Crap*, mister," she said, and then covered her mouth with her hand.

Maddox looked down at himself. The bruising covered half his side, with a swath of road rash across his stomach. "It's not as bad as it looks," he said, wishing (now that it was too late) that he'd managed to do a better job of hiding the extent of his injuries from the humans. As a shifter, he'd heal faster than they would believe.

"It looks awful," Bailey said. "Does that hurt much?"

"Not much," Maddox lied, trying not to breathe deeply. Then Verity dabbed at the road rash with iodine and he had to clench his teeth on a gasp.

"Mm-hm," Verity hummed noncommittally.

Maddox lowered his arm to try to keep what he was increasingly sure was a sprained wrist out of her sight, before remembering she couldn't see it. Bailey could, but she was too busy boggling at his bruised torso.

And not just at the bruises. She was also staring openly at his tattoos. Maddox had been getting ink for almost twenty years, and he had tattoos all over his torso, upper arms, and neck. An enormous dragon curled over his shoulder with its claws reaching across his chest, nearly meeting the horns of a powerfully muscled bull coming up from his ribs and lower-back area. A small-town girl like Bailey, in spite of her punk hair and attitude, had probably never seen tats like that.

Bailey noticed that he'd noticed her staring. She blushed sunrise-bright and looked away.

"I realize a half-naked man is an unusual sight around here, but I'd appreciate it if you'd hand me the pot of ginseng salve," Verity said.

"I wasn't looking," Bailey said quickly, taking two tries to pick up the jar by her knee. She darted a quick, anxious glance at her boyfriend. Maddox glanced at Luke, too; he didn't need a jealous teenage boy on top of everything else. But Luke was too busy boggling at the tattoos himself to notice.

Small-town kids, Maddox thought. He suddenly felt a hundred years old.

And he was intensely, vividly aware of Verity's hands on his torso. Her touch was firm but gentle, cleaning his wounds and spreading healing in their wake. The goo she rubbed on his road rash smelled sharp and spicy, tingling and then soothing.

He was also very, very aware that the more she touched him, the more he ... well ... the more glad he was that she couldn't see the effect she was having on him. The teens would have been able to, but they were both too busy trying to pretend they weren't looking at his tattoos to notice anything farther south.

"How's the rest of you?" Verity asked, and his blush flamed so fiercely that he could feel it all the way out to the tips of his ears.

"Fine," he managed.

"I trust that you're telling enough of the truth that you're not going to die in the night from a ruptured spleen."

"Nah," he said, getting a little of his breath back. "I just need to rest." Trying to be subtle about it, he reached for the edge of the blanket with his good hand and pulled it into his lap.

"Speaking of the truth, is anyone going to tell me what happened out there?" Verity asked. She was picking gravel out of his road rash now, which was painful enough to keep him from being too distracted by the way she bit her lip in concentration as she worked. Mostly.

"You're not going to like it," Bailey began hesitantly.

"Oh, trust me, I'm going to like *not* hearing about it a lot less."

The teenager puffed out her cheeks with a sigh and darted a glance at her boyfriend. "We were trying to help."

"Help whom?" Verity inquired. She reached for a pad of gauze and pressed it to Maddox's abdomen.

"You," Bailey burst out. "It's not fair what they're doing to you, Aunt Ver. What they're doing to this whole town. Luke and I just wanted to let people know what was going on."

Verity let out a long sigh that seemed to come from the bottoms of her feet. "And what exactly was this act of civil disobedience and family loyalty?"

"... Umm." Bailey looked at her boyfriend, but no help was coming from that direction. "We were adding a, um, a message to Sheriff Hawkins's reelection billboards."

"And by adding you mean—"

"Spray-painting," Bailey said in a tiny voice.

"And this message was?"

Bailey's nerve failed her and she looked at her boyfriend.

"One of you had better tell me."

Luke looked like he'd rather face the sheriff at this moment. "We painted, uh, 'The sheriff is a sellout.'"

"Luke misspelled Sheriff," Bailey said.

"Oh, c'mon! I put in the missing F after—"

"Was that all?" Verity interrupted, with an expression of long-suffering patience.

"We also painted 'Ducker plus Hawkins equals pay-offs'," Bailey said. "With, you know, the plus sign and all."

"And 'follow the money,'" Luke said. "Well, actually we used dollar signs because we were running out of billboard."

"And that's the point where we got caught," Bailey put in.

"Yes, of course you did. It's vandalism!"

"We just felt like the people needed to know!" Luke protested.

Maddox had never raised a teenager, but he'd been one, so he recognized Verity's "laugh or scream" expression. After she struggled to control her reaction for a moment, she said, "And that was when the sheriff and his men hit you, Luke?"

"Yes, ma'am," the boy said quietly. "They only hit me a couple of times. Mr. Maddox showed up then."

Both the kids were looking at Maddox with shining, worshipful eyes. He had to look away. If they only knew some of the things he'd done; he was no better than the sheriff's thugs. He wasn't anyone's hero.

"Ms. Breslin, please don't tell Grandma," Luke begged. "I told her I was going out to the lake with some friends. I'll be in *so* much trouble if she finds out."

"You're in trouble here too," Verity informed him with a sharp edge to her voice. "Bailey!"

"Yes, Aunt Verity?" came the meek response.

Verity plunged a hand into the deep pockets of the long, handmade-looking skirt she wore and came up with a couple of crumpled bills that she passed to her niece. "You two go down the street to the Whistlestop and pick up burgers for all of us. Straight there and back, understand? Do you want anything to drink, like a Coke or something?"

It took Maddox a moment to understand the last question was addressed to him. "No, thank you, ma'am. I could pay—"

"Don't," Verity said. "It's on us. It's the least I can do for you rescuing these two from their own stupidity. Bailey, get the double-decker bacon burger for him, will you? How do you like your burger?"

Bailey took their burger orders without complaint, and she and her boyfriend vanished out the back door. Verity began gathering up discarded gauze wrappings and other supplies, her hands moving swiftly to find them by touch. It was hard not to be distracted by the way she moved, that swift confidence that made him want to feel the assuredness of her hands on him again—

"How do you feel?" Verity asked him, jolting him out of thoughts that were rapidly sliding in a direction he'd hoped to stay away from.

"Better, ma'am. I appreciate you doing this for me."

Verity huffed. "You're the one who did me a favor, a huge one. Those idiot kids ... spray-painting graffiti on the sheriff's signs! What were they thinking?"

She got to her feet and lifted the pan of water. Maddox started to get up to help and sank back with a grunt of pain.

"Don't go anywhere," Verity said sharply. "I know you think I don't know how badly you're hurt. I just hope you're right that you'll be okay without a hospital."

"Just need some sleep to fix me up." With his shifter healing, it was more true than she knew. But he couldn't tell her that.

Instead he watched her move unerringly over to the sink against the wall, find the edge of it with her elbow, and pour out the water. Then she reached beside the sink, found an electric kettle by touch, and began to fill it.

"I expect you could use painkillers," she said. "I'll get you some aspirin when the kids get back with food—it's hell on your stomach otherwise—but in the meantime I'll make you some tea to help, one of my special blends for pain and fever."

Maddox wasn't really a tea drinker, but the lady had just patched up his wounds and was about to feed him; it wasn't like he was going to ask for coffee instead. Instead he said, "Thanks, ma'am," and watched, enraptured, her graceful movement from sink to counter, as she set the teakettle to heat and then turned and began running her fingertips across the jars.

"How can you tell what's in 'em?" Maddox asked.

"They're all labeled." She turned one of the jars toward him. It had a label stuck on the side, with lettering that he couldn't read from here, and fancy little bit of twine tied around the top with a slip of paper on it. "Bailey helps me with the labels for the customers, but this part also has it in Braille." She fingered the paper slip. "Of course, I can also tell by smell. I can recognize nearly ever kind of tea we carry by the way it smells."

Maddox looked around at all the racks of little jars. "Wow. There must be hundreds."

"More like thousands," Verity said absently, reading the labels with quick brushes of her fingertips. "Hmm, the willow blends should be on this shelf—oh, they're on the one under it. I need to talk to Bailey about moving things around." She unscrewed a jar lid, sniffed, nodded, and took it back to the sink.

"That's some nose you've got there," Maddox said, impressed.

"It's just specialized knowledge. Every trade has it. I'm sure there's something you know just as much about."

The comment was left dangling, inviting a reply, but there was nothing he could say to that. Nothing that wouldn't result in her kicking him out in the street. *Yeah, I know everything there is to know about different kinds of guns and how many times you can hit a person before they start to talk.*

Not the kind of influence she'd want around her niece.

Not the kind of influence who should *be* around her niece, for that matter. But he was hurt and he was tired and hungry and ... weak. He wanted to stay here in this cozy, nice-smelling tea shop for a little while longer.

"Is this your place?" he asked instead. "I mean, you run this place, right?"

"Lock, stock, barrel, and teaspoons," Verity said proudly, measuring tea into a small china teapot with flowers on it. "I own the building too. That's why Ducker—" She stopped. "But there's no reason to get into that."

"Who's Ducker?"

"William Ducker." She said it like a curse. "Silvermine's self-appointed land baron. He's buying up all the businesses along Main Street to turn this town into some kind of Ye Olde Weste tourist trap. Half the business owners in town have sold out to him already. If they won't sell ..." She shook her head and concentrated on pouring hot water into the pot. "The sheriff's in his pocket and so is most of the zoning board."

"I think I met him," Maddox said.

Verity, in the act of setting the electric teakettle back on the counter, turned toward him in astonishment. "What? When?"

"Earlier tonight. Older guy, silver hair, looks like he thinks he can snap his fingers and everyone around him is gonna hop to it?"

Verity leaned a hip against the counter and folded her arms. "I couldn't tell you about the silver hair," she said, and Maddox could have kicked himself; he'd forgotten that a visual description would mean nothing to her. "But that certainly sounds like him. Where did you see him?"

"He was there when the sheriff was beating the shi—uh—harassing the kids."

"That *bastard*," Verity snapped. "Pardon my language, but —*oh*. He likes to get Sheriff Hawkins to do his dirty work. I know the brick through my window was Hawkins, or one of his men, but threatening teenagers is going too far even for them."

"Someone threw a brick through your window?" Maddox bristled as inside him, his bull snorted its rage.

"It's not your problem." Verity sniffed the steam coming off the teapot and reached for a cup.

We will trample anyone who dares hurt her! his bull huffed.

Maddox kept his voice level with an effort. "Excuse me, ma'am, but you helped me when you didn't have to. I'd like to repay it if I can. These people shouldn't be bothering you."

"I appreciate the thought, but I'm afraid there's nothing you can do." She bowed her head as she spoke, her braids falling down to frame the cup as she poured hot tea into it. "Ducker is determined to get this piece of land, and he's got the money and clout to make it happen, one way or another. Especially with the sheriff in his pocket. We were hoping at the last election that we could finally get rid of him, but with Ducker's help he couldn't lose. I'm sure it'll go the same way this year. The law's on my side, but ..."

She shrugged, and her hopelessness broke his heart, especially contrasted against her confidence earlier.

But maybe now you have somebody on your side who knows about doing things the not-so-legal way, he thought, but didn't say.

The thought occurred to him that his old boss, Darius, might be able to help her, but he didn't want to ask. Darius had his own life, with a mate and a baby on the way. Maddox couldn't drag him into someone else's problems, in someone else's town.

He was going to help her. He couldn't just walk away, not after she'd helped him. But he meant to do it his way.

"Anyway, listen to me going on and on." Verity forced a smile and turned toward him with the cup of tea. "Here—be careful taking it, it's hot. If you like this, there's more in the pot if you want it—"

As she spoke, she reached down for his shoulder to get his location so she could put the teacup in his hand. But when her warm fingers settled on his bare skin, she froze, and so did he, with one hand in the act of reaching for the teacup. It was like an electric charge tingled through him at the touch of her skin, and for a moment he thought she must have felt it too.

"Oh," she said. "Oh, I can't believe I—your shirt, of course, it must have been dirt and blood all over, and you've just been *sitting* here—" It was the first time he'd seen her flustered; her cheeks were turning pink.

"It's okay," Maddox said hastily, taking the teacup before she dropped it on him. That was it, she was embarrassed as a hostess, and now he felt bad for her. It wasn't like he was even much of a guest. "I'm not really cold."

"I—I'll find something for you to wear," she said, and retreated toward the back of the store so hastily that she bumped into one of the racks of little jars and had to catch it as it began to teeter.

Left alone, he sipped at the tea. It was flowery and herbal and not at all his kind of thing, but it made him think of her. When he inhaled the steam, it was like breathing in the faint floral scent of her hair.

Sure she's not our mate? he questioned his bull.

Not sure, the bull repeated.

Dumb ox. Never could get a useful answer out of him.

VERITY

W hat was she thinking? Verity scolded herself. Letting the man sit around catching his death, and she nearly let him sit there half-naked through dinner as well, with her teenage niece in the room. Heavens.

Just the brush of his bare shoulder had sent warm shivers through her. She could still feel the touch of his skin against her hand.

What's the matter with me? He's a guest ... a guest I'm doing a very poor job of hosting.

She started to head for the stairs, but realized there wouldn't be anything in the apartment that would even come close to fitting him, based on what she'd felt of the width of his shoulders and chest. All that was up there was her and Bailey's clothes. Even if Luke had left something at their place (*And if he has, I'm having a word with his grandma,* she thought grimly), she didn't think a man Maddox's size could wear anything belonging to a teenage boy.

Wait! She had an idea. Rather than going upstairs, she went into the storeroom instead.

The store didn't sell much tourist stuff, but they did have a few souvenirs, including some Silvermine and Arizona T-shirts. Verity brushed her fingers over the boxes, reading the labels. Most of these were labeled using a label maker with raised lettering, so both she and Bailey could read them. Unfortunately, Bailey had done the labeling and hadn't put on anything about what the shirts actually looked like. But they did have the sizes on them. She picked an XXL just to be on the safe side—probably too big, but with his scrapes and bruises, loose was better than tight. And ... there was a box of hoodie sweatshirts around here somewhere too, wasn't there? She found an XXL among those, and went back to the shop with it.

"I'm coming back," she called, just in case he was ... well ... doing whatever men did when left alone in a tea shop. It wasn't like she thought he was up to no good, but ... she *had* left him alone with all her merchandise, come to think of it, and with the till. Any of her more sensible neighbors would probably say she was being a fool. They'd say he was faking the extent of his injuries, getting her to let her guard down.

But she trusted him, on a level she couldn't even explain. He'd intervened to save two kids from a bully of a sheriff. A man who did that kind of thing wasn't the sort of person who was going to steal money from a blind woman's cash register.

"Hi," he said, from exactly the place she'd left him.

"I brought you something to wear." She deposited the clothes in his lap. "How do you like the tea?"

"It's nice," he said promptly, which probably meant he hated it.

"It's good for you. Drink it all."

"Yes, ma'am," came the meek response, along with little rustles as he got dressed, which she tried not to think too much about, and especially not to think about the slide of the

37

T-shirt's soft folds over the hard planes of his chest and stomach that she'd felt earlier ...

Down, girl.

She was saved by the bell just then, or more accurately by the clatter of the returning teenagers, bringing with them the waft of warm, fragrant smells and a cheerful babble of conversation about the other teenagers they'd run into at the Whistlestop.

She and Bailey usually ate upstairs, in the small kitchen of their shared apartment, but Verity decided that the café corner of the tea shop where she kept the chairs and the couch would do just as well. It wasn't very big; she didn't serve food aside from a few packaged snacks, but she liked to have somewhere that customers could sit down, enjoy a cup of tea, and spend some quality time with a book or a laptop if they wanted to. Bailey had talked her into offering free wifi and helped her set it up.

With the cushions pulled down off the couch, they all sat on the floor and used the burger takeout boxes for plates. Verity put on some water to make more tea, and listened for the little rustles of their guest that let her know if he was calm, or fidgeting and nervous.

Sounded like mostly nervous. But he wolfed down the double-decker bacon burger and fries. Bailey had also brought back at least one chocolate milkshake (Verity could tell by the smell), and from the slurping of straws, it sounded like she'd brought one for Maddox as well.

In Bailey's eyes, it was clear, Maddox was the hero of the day.

And what do I think?

What she thought, or at least what some part of her thought, was that she wanted to get her hands all over that broad chest and lightly scruffy jaw, and find out just exactly how well-muscled and hairy the rest of him was. (Her imagination was happily providing answers to *those* questions.)

"What was that?" she asked, aware that Bailey had just asked a question.

"I said, Mr. Maddox can sleep in my room if he needs a place to stay."

"What? No!" Verity exclaimed, shocked.

"Not with me *in* it," Bailey said sulkily.

"You don't need to put me up, ma'am." The pitch of Maddox's quiet voice shifted as he turned toward Verity.

"Of course we will," she declared. "But not in anyone's bedroom." This was at least partly in response to her own treacherous libido. *There's plenty of room in* my *bed ...* "Will sleeping on the couch down here be all right? I can bring down some blankets."

"It'd be wonderful, ma'am. Thank you."

"Enough with this 'ma'am' nonsense. I patched you up, so I think we're on a first-name basis now—if that's all right with you, *Maddox*."

"Yes, ma'a—" he began, and then she could hear the smile in his voice when he changed it to, "—Miss Verity."

Which made her feel like a schoolmarm in an old Western. She could hear quiet snorting as Bailey and Luke tried not to laugh. "That's enough out of you two. Luke, I think it's about time you should be getting along home. You two didn't run into any trouble on your walk over to the Whistlestop, did you?"

There was a silence just long enough that Verity knew Luke had just responded in some visual way—a headshake, probably—before Bailey said, "No, Aunt Ver. We didn't see the sheriff or a single deputy's car."

"I'll go home the long way by the creek, just in case," Luke said.

"Good. Be careful. Bailey, run upstairs and bring down some blankets and a pillow."

The kids scattered, and Maddox said softly, "I don't want to put you in danger because of me."

"Trust me, you haven't," Verity replied just as quietly. "I was in danger long before you came to town."

She could sense him bristling at this, and his voice was a low growl. "Nobody's gonna hurt you or your family as long as I'm here."

"That's kind of you," was all she could say, overwhelmed by an unexpected surge of emotion. She had been on her own for so long—all her life, really. Her parents had always thought that her sister, Bailey's mother, took care of her since she was the blind one, but it was really more of the other way around, and now the rest of her family was gone and it was just her and Bailey. It had been long, so very long, since she'd had anyone to lean on ...

And you can't get used to it now, she told herself severely, even as her traitorous hands wanted to reach out for him. He was going to move on, if not tomorrow then sometime soon. She didn't need to let herself get attached to someone who was clearly just passing through.

But he was the one who reached for her: a light brush of callused fingertips across the back of her hand. "I'm not just sayin' that. I'll make 'em leave you alone, Miss Verity."

"It's not your problem," Verity protested, struck by the conviction in his voice.

He really sounds like he means it. But he doesn't understand how things work here. What does he think he's going to do, fight the entire sheriff's department and the richest man in town?

"It's my problem now," he said.

His scent was intoxicating, a heady male musk, tinged with hints of dust and iodine. She wanted to lean into it, bury her face in his neck and drink deeply of his smell and the tantalizing warmth of his skin.

Instead she pulled back, freeing her hand from the light touch of his. "I'm going upstairs for the night. There's a small bathroom in the storeroom, just a toilet in a closet, but it'll do for you tonight. Thank you ... Mr. Murphy."

And with that, she fled before she could embarrass herself further.

Upstairs, she went through her nightly routine while waiting for Bailey to come back, aware the entire time of unaccustomed sounds from the floor below: the toilet flushing, water gurgling in the pipes, faint thumps and rustles as Maddox got settled for bed. She stood in her bedroom, unbraiding her hair and brushing it out into a heavy cascade over her shoulders, and thinking the entire time of what it might feel like to have Maddox run those big, sure hands through her hair—brush it back from her face—stroke his callused thumbs along her jawline and draw her in for a kiss—

What is wrong with me?

It had been a long time since she'd had a crush. She'd just been so busy: with the store, with raising Bailey after her sister's drunk-driving accident, and now with this entire business with Ducker and the sheriff. There was no time for a love life, regretful as she might be about her youth passing her by. How was she supposed to go out and meet men, especially in a small town where she already knew most of the eligible bachelors and wasn't interested in any of them ...?

And she never remembered a crush as physically powerful as this one. At least not with someone who was, she had to keep reminding herself, a total stranger. He didn't *feel* like a stranger, was the thing. It was as if she'd known him before—in her youth, in a past life—and now it was like renewing a beloved old acquaintance rather than getting to know someone she'd never met.

It was like her soul had been pulling toward him for her entire life, except she'd never noticed it, in the way a fish doesn't notice the water around it ... until he was *there*, the other half of herself clicking into place.

How silly, she thought, brushing out her hair with smooth, regular strokes. *I don't believe in soulmates.*

But she couldn't help being very aware of every move he made downstairs, each creak of the floor and gurgle of water in the pipes. And when she went to bed that night, instead of putting on one of her usual audiobooks, instead she lay awake and listened to the soft sounds of building at night, its creaking and popping, the murmur of music from Bailey's headphones in her bedroom next door ... and distantly, muffled by the floor, the soft snoring of the stranger downstairs, who felt like no stranger at all.

MADDOX

He woke to the spill of morning sunshine across his face and the creak of footsteps moving about overhead. For a little while, Maddox lay wrapped in unfamiliar blankets, nose tickled by the spicy smells of the shop.

Sleeping on cushions on the floor while beat up black and blue hadn't been the greatest experience, but it felt like he'd actually gotten a pretty good night's sleep. His sore ribs protested when he carefully sat up, but it felt like his shifter healing had made a good start on knitting torn muscles and mending cracked bones. He took a few cautious, limping steps around the shop, trying not to knock into anything (with mixed success), and found that he could walk okay as long as he was careful. It wasn't all that different from normal, he thought with a grimace, or at least his new normal.

Fast shifter healing wasn't an all-around blessing. Sometimes you got things like what had happened with his hip, where the bones knitted into the wrong position. There wasn't really much to be done about it, short of rebreaking his hip and trying to rearrange everything, and he wasn't even sure if that would fix it completely. The muscles and ligaments and all those squishy, stretchy bits had rearranged themselves around his misshapen hip, and it didn't feel like they could ever go back how they'd been.

But his new injuries seemed to be healing straight. He did some cautious stretching. As long as he took it easy and didn't do anything strenuous for a little while, he figured he'd heal up fine.

Nothing strenuous. Like going after a crooked sheriff and the corrupt businessman who had the sheriff in his pocket.

It's none of your business. This woman isn't even your mate.

Or is she?

He still wasn't sure, and it puzzled him that his bull didn't know. He hadn't realized it was possible for a shifter to just ... not know. You either knew or you didn't. At least that was how he'd always thought it worked.

Maybe it was something to do with the fact that she couldn't see him?

Well, he thought, whether she was his mate or not, she had awakened his heart in its cold, lonely prison. He hadn't felt this much, this strongly, for another person since ... forever, probably. He had no intention of going away and leaving her to face this threat alone.

Quick, sure footsteps came creaking down the stairs.

Maddox glanced down at himself quickly, making sure he was decent-ish. The T-shirt she'd given him was bright blue, with an outline of Arizona and the word ARIZONA in brilliant red-and-gold-striped letters. And a cactus.

It wasn't exactly his normal kind of thing, and it was rumpled from being slept in, but at least it looked better than his jeans, which definitely had the look of a pair of jeans that'd been worn while getting hit by a truck and then rolling in a ditch. He had taken off his hiking boots before bed last night, so he had nothing on his feet but a pair of stained socks with a hole in the toe.

And then he remembered: oh right. She couldn't see him.

He was still scruffing a hand through his hair, trying to brush out the sand and get it as smooth as a brush-cut could get, when the back door opened and Verity came in.

Her brown-and-gray hair was done up in a single braid this time, wrapped around the crown of her head and pinned in place. She must have taken her braids out last night, and he wished he could see that—her hair kinked up from the braids, floating around her shoulders in a loose, silky cloud. Her blouse today was cream-colored and embroidered around the cuffs, and she wore a different long skirt, this one striped in wide bands of purple and blue and gold that made him think of a sunset sky deepening into night. She carried a tray with a cup and some other dishes on it.

"Maddox?" she said, tilting her head, and he realized he'd just been standing stupidly in the middle of the shop, not saying anything so she'd know where he was.

"Here," he said, and she turned her head quickly and smiled.

"Hi there. I brought you breakfast." She moved swiftly between the shelves, navigating more deftly in the crowded shop than he could do with two good eyes. But then, she must do it every day, so she knew where everything was.

"Smells good," Maddox said with automatic politeness, before the smell caught up with him and he realized that it really did. There was a bowl of oatmeal, a plate with bacon and eggs and two pieces of toast, and a cup of what he really hoped was coffee.

"We like to eat good breakfasts around here," Verity said, smiling at him. "I won't send Bailey off to school on half a bowl of overly sugared store-brand cereal that'll leave her hungry by the end of first period."

As if the name had summoned her, loud footsteps pounded down the back stairs. "Bye, Aunt Ver!" Bailey called through the half-open back door. "Hi, Mr. Maddox! Bye, Mr. Maddox! See you after school!"

"Keep a good lookout on your way there, and come straight home after!" Verity called to the retreating clatter on the back walk.

"She gonna be okay?" Maddox asked through a mouthful of toast.

"She'll be fine. I don't expect they'll try anything in broad daylight, with a lot of other people around. And she usually walks to school with her friends." But Verity was gazing in the general direction of the back door, frowning, eyes fixed on nothing. "I didn't mean to put my niece in danger with my own stubbornness. Maybe I *should* leave. Take her somewhere safe."

"You could do that," Maddox agreed. "But you'll always feel like you're running. That's no life for a kid either, having to look over her shoulder all the time."

"You sound like you know what you're talking about," Verity said quietly.

"Let's just say I've had some experience with moving around." He stuffed a piece of bacon in his mouth to stop himself from saying any more, but ended up saying around it, "You want some of this?"

"I've already eaten, but thank you." With that, Verity began moving around the shop, straightening things, putting the couch back to rights and folding the blankets.

"I can help with that—" Maddox began.

"No, you sit there and eat." She looked over her shoulder at him. He still kept forgetting she couldn't see; it really seemed like she was looking at him most of the time. "Did you sleep well?"

"Slept great. Thanks, ma'a—uh, Miss Verity."

Verity smiled patiently and gathered up the blankets. "When you're finished eating, can you take these upstairs for me? You're also welcome to use the bathroom up there and freshen up."

He stuffed the last piece of toast into his mouth and said around it, "I'm done." Except for the cup of what had turned out to be not coffee but tea. He wasn't going to be rude and ask if she had anything stronger, but he wasn't sure if he'd ever develop a taste for the stuff.

"You must have been hungry," Verity said. She sounded impressed. "Take the tray with you too, then, and if you could, I'd really appreciate it if you'd do the dishes while you're upstairs. You can just leave them in the sink. I'll put them away."

She held out the blankets and Maddox took them, struggling not to give in to temptation to let his fingers brush across her small, strong hands. "You don't mind me being up there alone?" he couldn't help asking.

"If I didn't trust you, I wouldn't have let you sleep in the shop last night. I'm a good judge of character, and I think you're a good man."

If she only knew what he *really* was. Maddox forced a smile, then realized she couldn't see it anyway. "Yes, ma'am," he managed to say, and balanced the tray on top of the blanket stack in one arm before picking up his cane and all but fleeing the shop.

The morning was already warm, the sky cloudless except for a few wispy trails of white near the horizon. Maddox climbed the back stairs slowly and carefully, with the cane tucked under his arm and his hand on the railing—noticing as he did so how the paint on the top slat was rough and peeling, and some of the rails were starting to loosen, nails jacking themselves out of the desert-dried wood. Maybe he could do a little work around the place while he was here, fix up a few things.

And take care of her corrupt-sheriff problem. If he could only figure out how to do that.

There was a small wooden balcony at the top of the stairs with a row of plants on the railing and a plastic deck chair. He freed a hand from the bundle in his arms to open the door. It led into a small but tidy kitchen, with a window over the sink looking down on the walkway wrapping around the side of the house, and the fence between Verity's shop and the house next door.

Maddox wasn't sure what to do with the blankets, so he left them in a neat pile on a kitchen chair. There were two of everything in the kitchen: two chairs, two cups and two spoons in the sink, two hooks by the door with a light wool coat hanging from one and a girl's jacket with sparkly rhinestones on the back hanging from the other.

Just Verity and her niece up here. He felt like an intruder already.

But he washed the dishes neatly and left them in the sink as she'd told him, leaving the tray on the counter since he wasn't sure where else to put it. He stuck his head down the short hallway off the kitchen. Two closed doors were probably the bedrooms, and the one open door led to the bathroom. Here again, there were two toothbrush cups (labeled with the raised lettering of a labelmaker: VERITY and BAILEY), and a small clutter of female things around the sink, hair brushes and a hair dryer and spray bottles and various electrical things with plugs that he knew had something to do with female hair but not exactly what.

She'd implied that he could use the shower, but he felt very weird doing that, so instead he used a washcloth to wash off the worst of the dust and leftover dried blood and iodine from last night. All the toiletries around the sink made him wish he had a toothbrush and deodorant. And that reminded him of his pack, still laying in the ditch if the sheriff hadn't done anything with it. *Need to go back and get that,* he thought.

Before leaving the bathroom, he examined himself in the mirror to see if he looked too disreputable. The scrapes and bruises were healing, and when he peeled off the bandages and tape from Verity's doctoring efforts last night, he looked passable—well, except for the tats, but there wasn't much he could do about those. He stood out in small towns wherever he went. He was used to it.

He didn't like the idea of Verity thinking he looked dangerous—but no, he reminded himself for the dozenth time, Verity couldn't see him. She only knew whatever his voice told her about him.

And anyway, he didn't think Verity seemed like a judgmental person. She was just ... nice.

Nice to others. Nice to be around. Nice-smelling—

Okay. Let's not go there.

He reminded himself he'd be leaving soon. He couldn't let himself get drawn too deeply into the lives of Verity and her family.

No matter how much he wanted to.

But at least he could leave their town a better place than he'd found it. That'd be a nice change from what he used to do for a living.

He splashed some water on his face, dried it on a clean towel, and dropped both towel and washcloth into the laundry hamper behind the door. On the way out, he noticed a few more things that needed fixing. The door stuck at the jamb, and the faucet dripped. Also, the gutter was sagging.

Good reason to stick around for a little longer, if Verity needed some things done around the place.

He made his way back down the stairs, moving a little less

stiffly now that he was starting to stretch out. On the back patio, he paused to look out over Verity's garden. He wasn't someone who cared about gardens much, but he was used to the tidy order of the gardens at his former employer Darius's mansion, with each bush neatly trimmed and all the flowers in matching colors.

This garden was very different. At first glance it looked like the backyard was simply overgrown, a wild riot of foliage and flowers with no particular pattern to it. Some parts of the garden were full of flowers, blazing in dozens of colors and spilling over the stakes and string tying them up; others were nothing but messes of leaves.

But then he thought, *Verity doesn't care what it looks like.* This must be where she grew the herbs to make her teas out of. And that made the garden suddenly look very different to him, not an unkempt mess but a garden full of useful plants, where every square foot was used for growing something. There were even plants in tin cans, cut-down milk jugs, and other sorts of containers sitting along the edge of the patio. Maddox leaned down and pinched one of the leaves, picking a plant at random since he didn't know what any of them were. It released a sharp, lemony smell that lingered pleasantly on his fingertips. Feeling slightly guilty, he nipped off the damaged leaf with his fingertips and dropped it on the nearby compost pile.

Verity wouldn't want to waste useful leaves by trimming her plants into ornamental shapes, the way Darius's gardener used to. This was a practical garden, not a garden for looks.

He really liked it here.

"Maddox?" Verity said, leaning out the backdoor.

"Here."

"Ah, I thought I heard you come down the stairs." She came out onto the patio, and he admired again how easily and gracefully she moved, neatly avoiding all the containers lined up along the patio's edge. "What are your plans for today? Did you have any?"

"I guess I was gonna go out and look for my stuff," he said. "I had a backpack. I lost it when the sheriff hit me with his car."

"That utter jackass," Verity muttered darkly. "Yes, of course you should do that. And if you're going out, would you mind doing some errands for me while you're at it?"

And so, somehow, without being sure how it had happened, he ended up leaving by the back gate with Verity's shopping list and a wadded-up reusable canvas grocery bag under his arm. He also had a tourist ball cap that she'd given him pulled down over his eyes. Maddox doubted it would help a whole lot—he was pretty recognizable—but it might at least help with the problem of having the sheriff's goons find him while he was out walking around.

Not that he *wanted* to hide. But he also recognized that he wasn't likely to win a fight in his present condition. Back when he was younger, he used to get into a brawl with every punk who picked a fight with him. But over the years he'd learned to fight smarter, to fight like a pro.

You didn't go into fights you couldn't win. You set it up to tilt things in your favor.

And I'm gonna win this fight. They're gonna pay for picking on these people.

He just hadn't figured out how yet.

I t took him awhile to find what he was pretty sure was the right stretch of road outside town, where the sheriff had run him down. He spent the walk looking around nervously for signs of sheriff's deputies or other possible trouble, but saw nothing.

And here I thought being a law-abiding citizen meant I was done having to look over my shoulders for the fuzz ...

Yeah, this was the right stretch of ditch; there were some brown blood stains on the rocks, and scuffed-up dirt and broken bushes where he'd crashed into the brush. Of his backpack, though, the only trace he found was his dented metal camp cup where it had rolled behind a rock. He'd carried it tied onto a strap on the outside of the pack; it must have fallen off.

Now where would they have taken it ...

C'mon, Maddox, that's not a hard question to answer. You gotta think like the goon you used to be. If he had been doing a job for one of his old employers, he would have made sure to clean up the area. Any personal objects left behind would be thrown away or burned.

Careless, he thought, looking at the blood on the rocks and the dented cup in his hand. Sloppy. The sheriff and this Ducker guy didn't have high standards. But then, he knew that already; they'd let him *and* the kids get away.

But then, they didn't have to be good at it. They were used to running a town where everyone was so intimidated that all they had to do was yell "Jump!" and the townspeople would ask "How high?"

Except for Verity and her family.

And there must be more people in town like them. They couldn't all have given in to this Ducker jerk's strong-arm tactics. One person alone couldn't win against people like that, but a bunch of them together ...

He slapped the tin cup into the callused palm of his other hand, then shook his head and put it in the canvas bag Verity had given him, and started walking toward town. He wasn't the kind of person people listened to, especially in a little town where he was a stranger and an outsider.

Verity might be able to. But he didn't know if he wanted

to try to talk her into it. Standing up to Ducker would be dangerous; that was the problem. That was why people didn't. There must be a lot of people here—most of them, in fact—who hated what Ducker and the sheriff had done to their town. But the nail that sticks up gets pounded down. As long as they kept their heads down and didn't get on Ducker's bad side, they could go on living their lives and raising their families in safety. Who, other than a couple of reckless kids, was going to risk their lives just to tell someone like Ducker "no"?

And who was he to tell them they ought to? He was a drifter with no family and no friends, a loner who'd probably be run out of town on a rail if his past came to light. He had no right to go around telling other people how to live their lives when he'd wrecked his own so thoroughly.

Still, he had to grin when he walked past a billboard for the sheriff with a couple of men in overalls industriously scrubbing the graffiti off the bottom edge. The sheriff's face grinned from the left-hand side of the billboard, bigger than life and twice as ugly. RE-ELECT SHERIFF HAWKINS ... EXPERIENCE COUNTS! read the enormous letters next to his face.

Maddox just wanted to plant his fist in that grinning mug.

And then, as he stood there looking at the billboard, an idea came to him.

Fight smart.

There was more than one way to defeat someone.

It wouldn't work, he thought. It was stupid to even think about it. All he'd do is paint a giant target on his back.

But ... if Ducker and Sheriff Hawkins were aiming at him, they wouldn't be harassing people like Verity. And maybe ... just maybe ... there was more than one way to get people to pull together in a crisis.

~

Despite the lateness of the season, it was punishingly hot by the time he got back to the tea shop, lugging a bag of groceries and leaning heavily on his cane. Neither his hip nor his recently injured ankle had appreciated all the walking. Neither did his ribs.

He went in the front so Verity would hear the tinkling of the bell. There were no customers in the shop, and Verity was at the counter with clean white paper spread in front of her and numerous little piles of crushed tea leaves.

"Hi," he said. "I got your stuff."

"Thank you so much. I'll take it upstairs as soon as I finish getting these sachets put together." She leaned under the counter and came up with a water bottle, frosted with condensation. "Thirsty?"

Now that she mentioned it, his tongue felt like it was stuck to the roof of his mouth. "Yeah. Thanks." He managed not to snatch it out of her hands, but instead took it politely and guzzled half of it in one go before going over and sinking onto the couch.

"It's incredibly dry here, and it can get to you fast. Not just the heat—it's getting cooler, now that we're getting on into fall—but the humidity and altitude as well. I forgot to warn you before you left, but I suggest carrying a bottle of water with you whenever you plan to be gone for awhile."

If this was what she considered cool, he'd hate to find out what "hot" was like. "I'll do that. Appreciate it."

Verity smiled as she sorted the tea. "Did you find your things?"

"Gone." He tried not to let it sting. It was just stuff. "Guess they wouldn't leave it laying there."

"Maybe someone else found it and picked it up. You might talk to the local newspaper office and see if anyone put an ad in. Or check the notice board at the Whistlestop. Everyone posts things there."

"No point," Maddox said. He rolled the empty water bottle between his palms. "Miss Verity—"

"*Please* call me Verity." She smiled again, mostly to herself, he thought. "I think after I've had my hands all over you, we can be on a casual first-name basis."

The memory of her sure, smooth fingers tingled through him. He had to adjust his position and get himself under control, forcing his mind back on track to continue. "Verity ... how would a person go about running for sheriff?"

Verity didn't look up—there was no reason for her to—but her head tilted in his direction to indicate her interest as she continued deftly sorting tea leaves. "Well ... I'm not sure. I guess you'd register with the county, probably at the courthouse, if the deadline's not already past. Why?"

"Well, I was thinking I'd sign up."

Verity's fast-moving fingers stopped. For a minute she just stayed like that, frozen in place. Then she said carefully, "You want to run for sheriff against *Hawkins*?"

"Yes, ma'am, I do."

"Maddox, I don't think you understand how dangerous Sheriff Hawkins is."

Maddox couldn't help snorting a short laugh. "He tried to run me over with his car. I know he's dangerous."

"He's run unopposed in the last three elections. If anyone makes the mistake of registering early on, they soon learn the error of their ways and drop out."

"I'm pretty hard to intimidate."

"If he can't scare you off, Maddox, he will try to kill you!"

"He already tried once," Maddox said. "Didn't take."

Verity hesitated. Then she got up from the counter. Brushing her fingertips across the counter's edge to orient herself, she came around the end and went over to him.

"Maddox." She touched the edge of the couch and sat down beside him. She smelled like the herbs she'd been sorting, fresh and green and a little spicy. "What you want to do for us ... I appreciate it. But I don't want to see you hurt or killed trying to do it. You're welcome to stay with as long as you need to, until you're feeling better and can move on. But you don't need to die for us."

"I'm not planning on it."

"Maddox—"

"Verity, listen." He took her hands in his, and the warmth of her skin was intoxicating, especially when she gripped his hands back. "I've known people like this Hawkins guy. Ducker too. You think they're gonna stop when they get what they want? People like that, they just keep wanting more and more. The only way you can get out from under 'em is to do like you said, sell your place and move away."

"Maybe I should." She let it out on a sigh. "I fight and fight, but I never seem to get anywhere."

"That's 'cause you've been fighting alone. Verity ..." He pulled her hands closer to him. "You're not alone anymore."

For a long moment she was still, her hands unmoving in his. Then without warning she leaned forward, lips parting.

Maddox met her halfway.

Her lips were impossibly warm and soft, tasting like vanilla and the sweetness of summer grass. *Tea*, he thought, with what little of him was capable of rational thought at that moment; *she tastes like tea.*

And she kissed like a woman who hadn't been kissed in a long time, tentative at first, then eager and wanting. She gasped against him, and he couldn't even think when he'd released his grip on her hands to instead take her face between his palms and curl his fingers around the smoothness of her pinned and braided hair.

The kiss broke at last, and she rested the side of her face

against his for a moment, her cheek impossibly smooth against his stubble. One of her hands rested tentatively against his side; the other had come to curve around his back. She was breathing hard, as if she'd run a race. "I think," she began. "I think—"

The bell on the door tinkled. Maddox looked up quickly to see the door starting to open, a shadow falling across the floor.

Verity jerked back, composing herself. As her face pulled away from his, Maddox heard her whisper a string of profanity that would've made a sailor blush. By the time the door opened all the way to admit an elderly woman with a shopping bag, she was back on her feet and fussing with the tea things, nervously picking them up and putting them down.

"Verity, dear? It's Flo Kendall. I'm here for the green tea and more of that lovely herbal blend."

"Yes," Verity said, somewhat breathlessly, patting at her hair. "Yes, of course."

She went to help her customer, but her fingertips brushed past Maddox's shoulder as she moved by him—merely orienting herself in space, perhaps, or perhaps a promise of more to come.

By the time she was finished with her customer, Maddox had managed to get a measure of calm back. *You're sure she's not our mate?* he thought at his bull. *Completely and totally sure?*

I told you, I can't tell, his bull retorted. *She smells very nice, though.*

She certainly did. And she felt nice. And she *was* nice. And she deserved much better than a guy who hadn't led a very nice life at all.

Or so he was telling himself when Verity came back over with a swish of skirts. He found himself leaning toward her, but she didn't sit down with him again. Instead she seemed almost angry—at him? At herself? "Are you still determined to do this?" she asked him.

"Yes, ma'am." At the very least, he could help this town deal with its corrupt sheriff problem before he left.

Verity let out a sigh and reached for the tea things. She seemed to be intentionally holding herself away from him. Had he upset her?

She's just worried, his bull said.

"If you're determined to do this," Verity said, "I suppose I can't let *you* do it alone either. Unless you know exactly how to go about running for sheriff ..."

"Not a clue," he admitted.

"You're going to need to file paperwork." She tapped her finger thoughtfully against her lip. "You could go down to the courthouse, but I expect you can probably do it online. Everything is online these days. You can use my computer."

"You have a computer?" he asked, surprised. Then, realizing how that sounded, "I'm sorry, ma'am. I didn't mean to imply you couldn't."

"Oh, I know," she said with a smile. "Most people are curious. Come around here."

She had a laptop on the counter, tucked behind a display of insulated tea mugs. It was a perfectly normal-looking laptop except it had what he at first glance took to be a second keyboard plugged into it, until he noticed the second keyboard had no keys except a few unlabeled ones at the top; most of it consisted of a wide strip with a bunch of tiny little dots.

"This is a Braille display," Verity explained, moving it to the side. "You won't need that." She tapped a key to wake up the computer. "Go on the internet," she told the computer, speaking clearly and loudly, and a web browser popped up. "I use voice commands along with the keyboard, and the computer reads things aloud to me. You can turn off the text-to-speech with this key." She brushed her fingers along the row of function keys -- all of them, he noticed, had additional labels pasted over the top -- and tapped one. "There, now you can use the internet without having it talk to you. Just put it to sleep when you're done."

She was as quick and sure with the computer as she was with everything else; it dizzied him. With that kind of energy and assuredness, what *couldn't* she do? "You ever think about running for office yourself?" he asked as she moved out of the way to let him access the laptop.

"Me?" Verity laughed. "What, run for *sheriff?*"

"Not sheriff. But maybe like, city council or mayor or something." He could imagine it so easily. She would look stunning behind a podium, wearing one of her pretty shirts and long skirts, her hair pulled back all tidy and professional. He bet she could get this town whipped into shape in no time.

Anyway, his bull put in, *we would stomp anyone who tries to argue with her.*

"Oh, heavens, no, what an idea. I don't want to run anything except my little tea shop." She started to reach for his shoulder, a casual touch—he got the impression she touched people a lot, but maybe she had to, to be sure where everyone was. As always, he wanted to lean into her touch like a flower toward the sun. But she pulled her hand back before her fingers made contact.

"Did I ... offend you?" he asked hesitantly. "Earlier?"

"What? Oh no, *no*. I just—I—" She took a breath. It was so odd to see her flustered. "It was very ... nice, and we'll talk about this a bit later," she declared, her cheeks turning pink, and her hand brushed his shoulder lightly in a fluttering kind of gesture before she hurried off to start moving teacups around in a display that had looked perfectly fine when she'd started with it.

Are you sure *she's not upset?* he thought anxiously at his bull. He had noticed over the years that people didn't usually say things like "I'm not offended" unless they actually *were* offended, but he was terrible at reading those things. At the same time, she didn't really *smell* upset.

It's not going to offend her any less if you assume she's lying to you, his bull told him.

Shut up, you're not any better at this stuff than I am. He turned his attention to the computer.

He wasn't that great at either computers or forms, let alone forms on computers, but he found the right part of the website fairly easily. It said the deadline for filing an application to run for sheriff was tomorrow. He hadn't even realized there would be a deadline. Now it almost seemed like this was meant to be, in a way. He didn't really believe in fate— aside from fated mates, of course, like anybody did—but he didn't make a single mistake in filling out the form, at least nothing he was aware of. He hesitated with his finger hovering over the "submit" button. Once he did that, there was no turning back.

Do I really want to do this? Do I want to get involved with these people's problems?

He looked across the store at Verity, who was moving a teacup a fraction of an inch to the left as if her life depended on it.

He couldn't just run off and leave Verity and her town in danger.

He clicked "submit."

The form whisked away into the depths of the computer, and Maddox sat back with a long sigh. Verity heard that, and stopped the teacup Tetris to come back over to the counter.

"All done," he told her. Now that there was no turning back, it felt like a weight had lifted from his shoulders.

"I hope you know what you're doing," she told him.

Maddox couldn't help grinning at her. "Not a clue, ma'am."

Verity shook her head. She touched the insulated-mug display with her fingertips, selected one, and placed it on the counter beside the computer with a tidy, decisive click. "One quarter," she declared. "In the cup. Now."

"What?" Maddox said blankly.

"From now on this is going to be the schoolmarm jar. Every time you call me ma'am, Miss Verity, or anything of that sort, it'll be a quarter in the jar."

She tapped the top of the cup meaningfully.

Meekly, he dug in his pocket and put a slightly grubby quarter in the cup.

Verity hadn't moved away. She was so close he could feel the warmth of her body and smell her soft, slightly spicy perfume smell over the nose-tickling scents of tea that filled the room. He could still feel the soft touch of her lips on his, the way she'd gasped and opened her mouth and her entire body had felt like it was on the verge of collapsing into his lap—

"Anyway," Verity said, jerking him out of a pleasant daze. "I need to put some orders together. Do you mind if I—since you're here, I mean, and don't take this the wrong way, but if you could use a little hired-man work, and if you're feeling physically up to it—*only* if you feel up to it, mind—would you mind terribly doing some things around the shop?"

He almost laughed, stopping himself at the last minute. "Like that loose railing on the stairs?"

"Yes," Verity said with a smile. "Exactly like that. There are some tools in the garden shed you can use."

"I was going to offer to do that anyway, ma—uh—"

"Quarter in the cup," Verity said, and her lips quirked, and he knew then that it didn't matter if his bull said she was his mate or not. He was head over heels anyway.

61

VERITY

Verity spend the afternoon filling orders to the background sounds of sanding and hammering and occasional tromping footsteps upstairs. She hadn't realized it would be so nice to listen to someone else around the place. It had been that way when Bailey was smaller, but now Bailey was a teenager on the edge of womanhood, and had her own life and friends; she wasn't home much anymore.

Verity found that she loved being able to pause in her work and listen, and pinpoint exactly where Maddox was and what he was doing by the sounds he made. There was hammering from the back steps: he was working on the railing. A sudden flush from upstairs: he must be dealing with that leaky pipe that had been driving her crazy with its drip, drip, drip for the last few months.

The only thing spoiling the pleasant afternoon was an intrusive, nagging worry. Sheriff Hawkins *really* wasn't going to like this.

But of all the people she'd met in this town, she thought Maddox might actually be able to take him on.

And she kept flashing back on the delightful memory of his beard scruff against her lips, the strength of his hands on hers ...

You're not alone anymore.

What was she doing? She was no starry-eyed girl to be swept away by a pair of strong hands and a chiseled, muscular chest.

(Such a very nice chest, though.)

You don't want to get too wrapped up in this one, Verity, she told herself, tilting her head to listen to his footsteps moving around upstairs as her hands went through the familiar routine of sorting and tying and packaging. *It might be harmless fun, but that's ALL it is. He's going to leave again. You know the type. You've spent your whole life with guys like this drifting through town. They come, they work on the ranches or the railroad for awhile, and they leave.*

But it didn't feel like that. It felt like a missing piece of herself, clicking into place.

And anyway, he wasn't like those other drifters. He was brave. There was no reason why he had to try to solve their town's problems; he didn't owe them anything. But he wanted to.

Some people were born heroes, Verity thought, and this town had had precious few heroes lately.

Bailey called around the time school let out to ask if she could go over to Luke's.

"Well, that depends," Verity said, cocking an ear for the sound of Maddox's footsteps moving around upstairs. "Are you actually going to be *at* Luke's, as opposed to running around town like a hoodlum?"

"Cross my heart, I swear. Luke's grandma invited me to dinner, and she also wanted some help sorting old baby clothes for donating to charity. I promised last week and then I forgot."

Verity laughed. "You're a good girl, Bailey."

Bailey gave a very teenager-ish snort, and then asked anxiously, "Will you be okay, Aunt Verity? Is Maddox still there?"

"He's still here." As she spoke, she heard the tromp of feet crossing the floor in the other direction, and then hammering from the upstairs balcony. He was fixing *everything* up there, from the sound of things.

"It makes me feel better, having him there," Bailey said. "I know we just met him, but he saved me and Luke. I trust him. And I like knowing that you aren't alone there."

"Me too," Verity said quietly. Bailey giggled, and a sudden suspicion occurred. "Bailey, are you going over to Luke's grandma's house to give me some time alone with Maddox this evening?"

"No, of course not," Bailey said quickly. "Oops, there's my ride, gotta go, bye!"

"Call me when you get there!" Verity said on the tail end of this, though she wasn't sure if Bailey heard her.

She hung up with a shake of her head. It seemed just yesterday Bailey had been a little girl, a patter of feet tagging after her in the shop and a small, sticky hand in hers. Now her little niece was growing up, figuring out her own path in the world.

And apparently matchmaking her aunt with her new favorite person.

Verity realized that she'd raised her hand to her head and was touching her hair to make sure the coiled braid was smooth, and then she had to grin at herself.

But why on Earth *shouldn't* she have some fun? She was barely even middle-aged; she certainly wasn't dead. Maddox hadn't seemed to object to their kiss earlier, and he was going out of his way to help with the town's corrupt-sheriff problem *and* with all the little issues around the

64

shop that she'd just been dealing with rather than getting fixed.

Decisively, she got up, marched over to the door, and flipped the sign to CLOSED. She locked the door and went out the back.

Dry heat met her, although the back porch was in shadow at this time of day. It wasn't the blistering heat of summer, but they were still having a warm fall. She hoped one of the things Maddox had fixed was the window-mounted air conditioning unit; being an upstairs apartment, their place trapped all the heat of the day. She didn't hear hammering at the moment. "Maddox?" she called. "Okay to come up?"

"Of course, ma—" and then he broke off and she heard him curse.

Verity smiled to herself as she climbed the stairs. "Another quarter for the jar, then."

"Next time I go downstairs," he said, resigned. "Oh, stop there!" She froze in the act of lifting her foot to the next step. "Where you are there, that's where I fixed the railing. How's it feel?"

Verity ran her hand up and down. The wood was smooth, without a single splinter or wobble. "You did a wonderful job. What else did you do?"

"Everything you told me about." As he spoke, he came down the stairs to meet her halfway. "Got the railing, got the leaky pipe and the air conditioner—" Which now that he mentioned it, she could hear humming away upstairs. "Smoothed down the place where the door used to stick, fixed a couple of loose boards on the deck—oh, and I fixed a little bit of a wobble in your kitchen table."

"You are a wonder," she told him. "I didn't even have to tell you about half those things."

"I'm pretty good at fixing stuff." His voice sounded strange when he said it, almost ashamed.

"What's wrong?"

"Oh, it's just ..." Maddox hesitated. "I haven't been doing things like that much lately. I think I'd like to do it more. Fixing things, I mean, and not ..."

He stopped. Verity didn't push. You could tell when people didn't want to talk about things, and she'd been around the block too many times to force it.

Instead she said, "You'll be staying for dinner, won't you?"

"If you'll have me," he said, suddenly shy again.

She had reached out and touched him before she'd realized she was going to, a light brush of fingertips across his arm. "Of course."

There was a lingering moment before he pulled away abruptly. "So—it looks like one corner of your shed roof is sagging pretty bad. I was just gonna go fix that for you, if you want me to—?"

"Yes, you can do that while I start dinner," she said, and his footsteps receded down the stairs, with a hitch every time he took a step that hurt him. She thought about calling after to tell him not to overdo it, but decided not to; his pride probably wouldn't appreciate it.

But still, she waited and listened to him go down the stairs before she began to slowly climb, alert with her toes for any tools that had been left behind. He seemed like the sort of person who would be tidy about his tools, but she'd spent much too long drumming into Bailey to pick up things off the floor not to worry that a stranger might not remember that she couldn't see objects before she tripped over them.

A wave of cool air greeted her when she opened the door to the kitchen. The air conditioner was humming away, much more quietly than it used to. Verity disliked having it running because its white noise covered up the smaller

66

sounds she relied on, but it was better than sweltering in late-summer heat.

She ran her fingertips over the labeled packages of frozen meat in the freezer, most of it obtained from local farmers. Thaw the chicken? No ... perhaps she'd make a pot roast. There would be time for it, if they didn't mind eating a little late, and it seemed like a nice thing to splurge on, and something he might enjoy. The oven would heat up the apartment, but with the AC running, it would be cool again by bedtime.

Once she had that in the oven, she moved around the apartment, tidying. Not that it was a mess to begin with. She'd built a lifelong habit of meticulous housekeeping; it was the only way she could always know where to look for the things she needed.

Despite all his banging around up here, Maddox had left everything exactly as he'd found it, right down to the position of the salt shaker on the table and the morning coffee cups that he'd left in the sink while doing his dishes. A point in his favor, she thought, smiling. She wasn't sure if he understood *why* everything needed to be left where it was, but he respected her things. She liked that.

She liked *him*.

Thinking about that, she went into her bedroom. *Would it be ridiculous to—oh, why not?* She changed the sheets on the bed and bundled the used sheets into the laundry hamper. Why not be prepared? She found herself feeling slightly self-conscious and hoping the sheets didn't have, say, cartoon kittens on them or something like that. (Bailey had bought them. Verity had never actually asked what they looked like.)

She changed into a clean shirt, one of the cool, silky ones she liked best. Color didn't matter to her, but fabric textures did; it was almost time for soft knit sweaters again, as the weather turned cooler, but this warm evening was perfect silk-shirt weather. And then she undid her hair from the braid. She brushed and brushed it, until it floated in a soft cloud over her shoulders, as silky smooth as the cool folds of her shirt.

Her small number of jewelry items were kept in a bowl on her dresser, carved from a piece of knotty pine—a gift from her sister, a long time ago—and covered with a handkerchief to keep the dust out. She liked jewelry that felt good to her fingers and had a nice weight against her skin. Running her fingertips over the contents of the bowl, she picked out a squash-blossom necklace and a pair of teardrop-shaped earrings that she clipped to her ears.

Feeling fancy and a bit silly, she toed off her shoes and padded barefoot across the cool floors into the living room. The roast smelled good and she knew from experience that it wouldn't need to be checked on until the timer went off. Verity got her audiobook player from its shelf and went out onto the balcony.

It felt luxurious to take the afternoon off, like playing hooky from school. She sat on a deck chair with her bare feet curled under her and the audio player in her lap, but she didn't put in the earbuds. She was perfectly contented just to sit here and soak up the sounds from around her: children shouting and laughing in neighbors' yards, a radio playing somewhere down the street, and Maddox's intermittent hammering noises from below. The balcony was in shade, the dry autumn heat pleasant after the baking oven of summer.

After awhile, Maddox's footsteps mounted the stairs. She already knew him by his steps, the same way she knew Bailey. The footsteps faltered and slowed as he neared the top of the stairs, and then he said, quietly, "Wow."

"Wow?" she asked, turning her face his way with a smile.

"You look ..." He stopped and took a breath. "I mean, you always look good. But you look ... *wow*."

No one had ever told her that she looked good before. It was sudden and startling and it took her breath away. She didn't actually *know*—if she was pretty, if she was plain, or somewhere in between.

She wasn't quite sure what to say in reply. *You too?* He did, to her, but people always reacted oddly when she said things like that. *But Aunt Verity,* Bailey had said when she was a little girl and Verity, braiding her hair, had told her what pretty hair she had (it was so smooth and soft, running through her fingers), *you can't SEE me!*

Maddox broke the silence by clearing his throat. "So this nice T-shirt you gave me ... I kinda got it all sweaty."

Verity laughed. "Go downstairs and get another one from the storeroom. Pick out whatever you like. We have plenty and they don't sell very well. I also wouldn't object if you wanted to use the shower."

She could hear the smile in his voice as he said, "Are you saying I stink?"

He definitely did *not* stink. She could smell him, but it was a pleasant masculine smell from hard work and exercise. "I just think you might be more comfortable that way. I know how much I appreciate a quick shower to cool off after working in the garden. Oh," she called as his feet went down the stairs, "and make sure to drink some water!"

His voice floated back up the stairs. "Yes, ma—Right, got it, that'll be two quarters in the jar. Right away."

MADDOX

addox took his time in the shower, scrubbing himself with shampoo that smelled like girls—a nice smell, floral and perfumey. He felt a little weird smelling like that, but he wanted to smell nice for Verity.

Fast shifter healing had reduced the scrapes to mostly-healed pink lines on his skin, the bruises to faded yellows and browns. His ribs still hurt sharply when he twisted wrong, and he had to step carefully on his injured ankle and take it a little easy on his wrist. But he was feeling a lot better despite having probably overdone it a bit today. For a human, it would be like the hit-and-run had happened a couple of weeks ago, rather than yesterday.

His body needed to replenish itself from somewhere, though. He was really looking forward to the roast he could smell cooking all over the house.

He put on the clean T-shirt he'd picked up downstairs, another tourist one with a prospector leading a donkey, and climbed back into his stiff, dirty jeans. If the sheriff had gotten rid of his pack (definitely what *he* would have done, in that situation), he was going to have to buy new pants before too long. And socks. In fact ... thinking of Verity's bare feet (long beautiful feet, peeping out from under her skirt), he decided to leave his shoes off and go barefoot around the house this evening.

Where all this was leading to, he wasn't sure. He knew where he wanted it to lead, but he was also scared to push it. He was a bull, charging into things without thinking them through. But this was too important. He needed to take it slow and careful, not trample or wreck things, just ... let it go where it was going to go.

When he came out of the bathroom, Verity was just taking the pot roast out of the oven, her hands encased to the elbows in the longest oven mitts he'd ever seen. He stopped in the kitchen doorway, not wanting to disturb her in the middle of dealing with hot dishes.

And also because he wasn't sure if he could have said anything if he'd wanted to. When he first saw her, she'd made him think of an angel, and the effect was even stronger now: the gorgeous cloud of gray-laced brown hair, the drifting skirt brushing the ankles of her bare feet ...

Except she wasn't, of course. She was a woman, a very beautiful woman, and part of what made her beautiful was how down-to-earth she was. Her bare feet were smudged with dirt and the hem of her skirt had grass stains, so he guessed she'd been down in the garden for a bit while he was in the shower.

"That's you, right?" she said over her shoulder, and he jumped. "I was thinking we could eat outside if you want to. It's so nice out there. It'll mean dishing up our plates in here, since there's not much room on the balcony and I don't really want to carry this roasting pan all the way down the stairs."

"Eating outside sounds great." Eating inside sounded great too, as long as she was there.

"Could you get some plates out? Top cabinet beside the sink. Just two plates," she added as she set the dish on top of the stove. "Bailey won't be eating with us tonight. She's over at her boyfriend's folks' house."

Just the two of them. He wouldn't have minded seeing her niece again, but his heart leaped at the idea of having an evening alone with her.

"You're probably wondering about the oven mitts," she remarked, stripping them off. "Bailey sewed these for me, because I kept accidentally burning my arms when I was cooking. It's all too easy, when you deal with the world mainly through touch, to brush up against things that you shouldn't have."

"It must be hard," Maddox said without thinking, then backpedaled. "I mean, not that you aren't good at it. And stuff."

"Well, it *is* hard in some ways, of course." She picked up the roast with a pair of barbecue forks and transferred it briskly to a serving dish for slicing. "Of course I wouldn't say it's not. But it's also just how my life is, you know? I've been blind since birth. I've never known any other way to be."

"That makes sense to me." He thought about being a shifter, which did complicate his life in various ways, but he also couldn't imagine giving up his shifter animal. With his bull only in occasional contact with him and his ability to shift in question, he felt like half a man. He couldn't imagine having it gone completely.

"Bailey wants me to look into getting surgery done. They can do amazing things these days. But I don't even know if surgery could help me, and I've also read that people who regain their eyesight as adults can't always learn how to see properly anyway. Your brain doesn't know how. You have to learn it, and some people never learn. I might trade the world

72

I know for a confusing world of shapes I don't know how to interpret, and who wants that?"

"It doesn't seem to slow you down," Maddox said as she reached for a plate, and Verity laughed.

"I try not to let it. Here, dish yourself up and we'll go down and eat in the garden. Could you do me a favor and bring the pitcher of lemonade from the fridge?"

She navigated the stairs with no visible difficulty, a plate in one hand and her skirt held up with the other. Maddox heaped his plate with roast beef and potatoes, then followed more slowly. He'd been getting around fine without his cane in the apartment and garden (the cane was downstairs, leaning against the wall of the shop) but descending the stairs with both hands full took some concentration. His hip and ankle both ached; his ribs twinged whenever he moved. He really had overdone it today.

But he felt good about it. This had been a day well spent; he was tired, but satisfied. He really *was* good at fixing things. He'd almost forgotten that.

He found Verity waiting for him in the garden, at a patio table with two plastic chairs.

"I love this time of day the best," Verity said as he sat down. She poured two glasses of lemonade, finding the rim of the glass with her fingertips. "Especially at this time of year, when it's not so hot and it's nice to be outside. It's just so peaceful. Bailey says the shadows in early evening look purple to her, and I think this time of the evening just feels ... purple. That's the best way I can describe it."

Maddox looked around at the garden drowsing in the last rays of the evening sun, a riot of flowers and foliage, seemingly out of control but actually obeying an internal sense of order that became more apparent the more he looked at it. Bees hummed lazily in the sun-drenched air, and there was a hint of coolness taking the edge off the heat of afternoon.

"It's really pretty," he said, and then felt immediately guilty because she couldn't see it; did she mind him saying that?

But she just smiled and said, "Yes."

They ate in silence for a little while, and Maddox could feel the peace of this place seeping into his bones, soothing away tension and stress he hadn't even been aware he was carrying around. The injustice of someone wanting to drive Verity away from here seared him to the bottom of his soul.

"Are you sure you're feeling all right?" Verity asked as the sun slipped below the rim of the world and dusk began to gather in the corners of the garden. "You seemed in such bad shape last night, but you've been working all day."

"It's okay. Helps keep me from getting too stiff." He looked down at the plate, where he'd demolished an enormous heap of pot roast. "Hope you weren't counting on leftovers, though."

Verity laughed.

"So ... you mind if I ask a kinda personal question?" Maddox said after a minute.

"Sure. Go ahead."

"I was just wondering about Bailey. She's your niece, right? How'd she come to live with you?"

"Oh, yes, Bailey. My little butterfly." Verity smiled, her eyes crinkling at the corners, but it was a wistful smile. A sad smile. "Her mother, my sister, had ... a troubled life, I guess you'd say. She wasn't a very happy person. She drank a lot, did drugs off and on, and Bailey's father was *not* a nice man. Thankfully he's in prison now and not a part of Bailey's life at all. Several years ago, my sister was in a drunk-driving accident, and she ... didn't make it." By now the smile had faded completely, leaving her face bereft, her eyes damp.

"Jeez." Words seemed inadequate. "I'm so sorry."

"Me too," Verity said, her voice soft. "She had such a hard life. I always hoped she'd turn it around, but she never seemed to be able to. But she loved Bailey, and we had already drawn up paperwork to make sure that Bailey would come live with me if anything happened to her. Bailey and I were already close, so I made up the second bedroom for her, and I haven't had a single regret ever since. She's a sweet girl and she's growing into a wonderful young woman."

"Her boyfriend seems like a good kid, too."

"He is. I don't have any worries about her when she's with him ... well, unless both of those two let their hearts run away with their heads and get into well-intentioned idiocy like the other night. But at least I know if they get hurt, it'll be trying to do the right thing." She topped off their lemonades from the last of the pitcher's contents. "I'm so glad you were there for them. That could have gone very badly, otherwise."

"You think he's gonna come after them again?" Maddox asked.

"I don't know. I think probably not. He'll be too busy coming after you." She grimaced. "Maddox, *please* be careful. These people don't like it when someone stands up to them."

"I know." He knew all too well. He'd been on the other side of it, doing dirty work for men like Ducker. "But that's when someone's got to."

hey took their dishes inside and cleaned up quietly, moving around each other in the small kitchen. It was shockingly easy to fall into sync with Verity, needing no words, scraping plates and handing them to her where she stood at the sink, taking the containers of leftovers she passed him and putting them away in the fridge.

He was very aware of her warmth and curves as she brushed past him. In the kitchen's close confines, they could barely turn around without touching each other. Her skirt whispered past him; her long hair brushed his arm as she turned to put the dishes away; her hip touched his thigh and then moved away.

It was not flirtatious; it was more than that. It was a sense of growing energy between them, the electric awareness that they were building toward something, and they both knew what it was.

She turned around from the sink just as he turned from wiping down the table, bringing them suddenly face-to-face, bumping into each other in a soft collision. Verity laughed quietly and raised clean-washed hands smelling of dish soap, not to push him away but to lay her palms against his chest through the T-shirt. She tilted her head back, her hair tumbling in a smoky cascade down her back.

When he hesitated—overwhelmed by her nearness, by the sweet female scent of her—she said with a hint of impatience, "So am I completely misreading the signs here, or are you planning on kissing me?"

Her lips were honey-sweet. His first kiss was a gentle sip, but she wrapped her arms around his shoulders and he placed a hand at the base of her spine and pulled her against him. Their kisses grew heated and frantic, Verity half climbing him with her bare foot pressed against his thigh.

"Bedroom?" she gasped, breaking the kiss, and he laughed out loud against her lips and swept her up, lifting her with hands cupped beneath her sweet round buttocks. She laughed too, wrapping her legs around his waist.

He carried her down the hall, still kissing her frantically, hungrily. The ache in his hip and the lingering discomfort of his healing bruises receded until he barely felt it for the heat coursing through his body. Through her rucked-up skirt he could feel the strength of her muscular thighs flexing against him. As soon as he laid her on the bed she began wriggling out of the skirt, while he stripped off the borrowed T-shirt and followed with his pants, leaving them crumpled on the floor.

Verity was unbuttoning her blouse now. Maddox knelt on the bed and put his hands over hers. "Let me do it."

He undressed her like unwrapping a gift. Her skin was glorious, sweet and smooth; he kissed every inch of her shoulders, her breasts, the curve of her stomach, with pauses to sample her sweet lips in between.

When he came to her at last, pressing into her silken heat, she rose to meet him with a gasping cry. Her body worked against him, sweat glistening on her skin as he thrust into her and she gave small, delighted moans that drove him to greater and more intense heights.

She clenched around him and that pushed him over the edge, and as he came, something seemed to wake inside him —like a connection snapping into place, a circuit closing, a half-finished sentence finding its ending.

He sank down slowly onto her, propping himself on his elbows to avoid putting too much weight on her, and as he gazed down at her blissed-out face and half-closed gray eyes, all he could think was: *Mate.*

She *was* their mate. And now he felt it, with over-whelming intensity.

Why didn't we feel this before?

Maybe because she couldn't see us, we couldn't see her? His bull seemed equally baffled.

Whatever the reason, it was there now—and he now understood why mated shifters spoke of it as an undeniable and unquantifiable thing; he knew why they said things like *You'll just know.* Because he *did* just know. This woman was the one for him, always and forever.

He rolled off to curl beside her, taking her gently into his arms. She ran a hand lightly over his chest and collarbone and shoulders, as if she was mapping his skin with her fingers—and that was, he realized, exactly what she was doing.

"Too fast?" he asked into her hair, and she burst into a girlish giggle.

"Just fast enough. You have no idea how long it's been since—well. Since." Her hand moved lower, stroking across his ribs, his hip; her fingers lingered over the ridges of the mostly healed road rash. "I keep forgetting you were in a hit-and-run just a couple of days ago. I don't want to hurt you."

"It was fine. I heal pretty fast. I always have."

"You must." She touched his side again. "It hardly even feels like you were hurt at all."

This conversation was starting to stray too close to things they were going to have to talk about eventually—but not now. Not tonight. Not when he'd only just found his mate, and had her warm, soft nakedness cradled in his arms. "How 'bout you? I didn't hurt you, did I?"

She giggled again. "Trust me, those were definitely not noises of pain." She pressed her lips lightly to his collarbone. "And I'm really not sleepy yet. I suppose you couldn't possibly be ready again, but—"

"You'd be surprised," he said, and rolled her over, to the delightful sound of her startled, happy laughter.

VERITY

Verity woke to the delicious warmth of Maddox curled around her, his scent and the tickle of his stubble against her cheek.

It was a Saturday, so she didn't have to get up early to open the store; on Saturdays she didn't open until noon. In fact, she didn't have to be anywhere. She drowsed pleasantly until she heard Bailey moving around in the kitchen, the creak of footsteps and the sound of running water.

She'd heard her niece come back last night, shortly after she and Maddox had settled down to sleep, but she hadn't thought at the time about the inevitable Walk of Shame when she emerged from the bedroom—especially since she'd been working hard to model good behavior now that Bailey was becoming a young woman and getting interested in boys.

On the other hand, "it's okay because I'm an adult and you're not" was a perfectly acceptable excuse, she decided.

She got up quietly. Maddox didn't stir. Verity wrapped herself in a bathrobe and went into the bathroom for a shower. While she was at it, she checked their box of backup bathroom supplies—something she'd gotten in the habit of keeping on hand over the years; there was no telling when a toothbrush was going to fall into the toilet or the Tylenol bottle turn out to be empty at the worst possible time, and not being able to drive plus having a business to run, she couldn't just dash out to get more. There was a spare toothbrush, still in its package, and an unopened tube of toothpaste, and she laid both on the edge of the sink for Maddox.

Washed and dressed, with her hair down to dry, she padded into the kitchen. "Good morning, Bailey."

"Morning," her niece's voice said from the table. There was a rattle and crunch of cereal.

Verity filled the electric teakettle and put it on to heat. "How was your evening at Luke's place?"

"It was nice. Say, Aunt Verity," Bailey said, "is Mr. Maddox still here?"

Verity went for a noncommittal, "Yes. He is."

"Oh good," Bailey said. "A courier dropped off a package for him this morning."

"A package for *Maddox*?"

"I know, right? They brought it right to the store. It's got his name on it and everything."

Verity felt a fat manila-sized envelope shoved into her hands. She pushed it back in Bailey's direction. "This is no help to me. Who's it from?"

"County clerk's office."

"Oh," Verity said. She got a tea mug out of the dish drain. "Oh ... yes. That must be paperwork for the sheriff job."

"For the *what*?"

Verity ran her fingertips across the tea labels in the cabinet. Today, she felt, was going to require caffeine. "Maddox is running for sheriff."

"He's doing *what*?"

Just then water ran in the bathroom, and the toilet flushed. Verity busied herself making tea.

"Aha!" Bailey declared. "I *knew* he wasn't down in the shop this time! You do *not* snore that loudly. You *go*, Aunt Verity. Fistbump!"

Verity sighed and held out her fist. Bailey's knuckles connected in a light tap.

"No, but seriously," Bailey said. "Good for you. Now what's this about the sheriff?"

The shower began to run. "Maddox can tell you himself when he's up," Verity said, opening the freezer. "Is there any bacon left?"

"You're making a proper breakfast? You must have it bad."

"Hush and get me the small mixing bowl."

By the time Maddox's footsteps creaked in the hall, she was busy scrambling eggs while Bailey kept an eye on the sizzling bacon. Verity heard Maddox's steps hesitate at the domestic kitchen scene, and said over her shoulder, "Good morning. Come on in. Do you mind wheat toast? We're a brown-bread household."

"Toast sounds great. Uh ... I don't suppose you have coffee?"

"Oh, *no!*" Bailey said in her most melodramatic voice. "How will this relationship ever work out?"

"Hush, you. There's very strong Irish breakfast tea in the upper cabinet. Bailey, could you get him down some? And maybe some of the chicory as well."

"It's not the same as coffee, Aunt Verity, I hate to break it to you."

"No, but it's the closest thing we have. Oh, Maddox, Bailey says there's a package for you."

"For me?" Maddox said, startled, as Bailey started banging around with the tea things.

"From the county clerk. I expect it's to do with the election. Bailey, that bacon's getting overdone."

"Get the tea, Bailey, get the bacon, Bailey—I don't have

twelve arms, Aunt Verity!" But there was renewed sizzling and the sound of bacon being transferred to the paper towels they'd set out on a plate earlier.

"Imagine shopping for clothes if you did," Verity said. "Would you buy six shirts, or one shirt with twelve arms? And wherever would you find it?"

"The internet," Bailey said complacently. "Or I could make my own. I'm *very* good with a sewing machine, Mr. Maddox. I made those oven mitts for Aunt Verity, and that apron, and —um—" From the sound of her voice, she'd turned around to talk to Maddox at the table, slotted spoon no doubt still in hand.

"Don't let that bacon spoon drip."

"How do you *do* that?" Bailey said. There was more sizzling and the click of the spoon against the draining plate.

"Experience, dear. Do you want two slices of toast?"

"What's in the envelope?" Bailey wanted to know. "Uh, yes, please."

"That's his business. Two slices or four, Maddox?"

"Four, thank you, ma—uh, Verity."

There were some small rustles that indicated Bailey had slipped over to the table to take a peek at the papers Verity could hear rustling around over there. "Bailey—"

"It's okay. It's just paperwork and stuff," Maddox said. "Actually ... I'm not so good with this kind of thing. I was gonna ask if you could give me a hand."

"You're really running for sheriff," Bailey declared. "Oh my gosh. You're *awesome*, Mr. Maddox. You'd be so much better a sheriff than Mr. Hawkins. Oh wow."

"I ... guess I hadn't thought that far ahead." Maddox's voice sounded slightly stunned. And Verity realized that it hadn't sunk in for her until that moment, either. She'd only been thinking about getting rid of Sheriff Hawkins—or, more accurately, thinking about his likely reaction to being challenged.

But if Maddox won the election, he'd be the sheriff for a full term.

He'd have to stay.

Let's not get ahead of ourselves here. "Is there room at that table for food, by any chance?" she asked.

The paperwork was moved aside, Bailey brought in an extra chair from the deck, and they dug into a hearty breakfast. Bailey kept up a steady stream of chatter; she'd clearly jumped into the idea of Maddox's election campaign with both feet, as Verity's mother used to say, and Verity quickly got the impression that Bailey was violating the "no phones at the table" house rule to look up election information online. As it was something of a special occasion, she decided to let it slide.

"You're going to need an election headquarters and signs and buttons and a *website*—"

"I don't think I need all that stuff, do I?" Maddox asked.

"I doubt it," Verity said. "The important thing is getting the word out that you're running. I expect people in this county would vote for a can of Spam instead of Ted Hawkins at this point."

Bailey giggled. "Oh, he should talk to the newspaper, then! And I can get Luke's grandma to spread the word. She knows *everybody*."

"I think you've found your election campaign manager," Verity said to Maddox. There was little room at the small table for more than two people, so he was sitting very close to her, their knees touching under the table. She didn't mind in the slightest.

"Can I?" Bailey declared. "It can be extra credit for poly-sci. Actually, I bet I can get university credit on this—"

"Let's take this one thing at a time," Verity said, laughing.

"I like your idea of talking to the paper. We can call them after breakfast. Actually, I see no reason why the store has to open today at all. Maddox, I think today is the day we get your campaign into full swing." She reached out and found his hand on the table. After a frozen moment, he turned it over and squeezed her fingers with his thick, callused ones. "If you're all right with it. Don't let us pressure you into anything."

"I don't feel pressured. Heck, you were trying to talk me out of it just yesterday."

"Oh my God, you guys are so *cute*," Bailey said.

"I know who's doing the dishes this morning," Verity said dryly.

"But I have to help Mr. Maddox with his paperwork," Bailey said, all innocence.

Verity smiled and got up, removing the plates.

"You do need buttons, though," Bailey said very seriously. "You can't have a campaign without buttons, and signs and stuff."

"I can't really afford that," Maddox said, sounding a bit nervous.

"Well, then you need to have a fundraiser. That's what campaigns do, right, Aunt Verity? They have fundraisers and get donors and stuff."

"He's running for sheriff, not for the state senate," Verity said.

"Well yeah, but he's running against Mr. Hawkins, who's got all of Mr. Ducker's money and all those signs. Oh, I have an idea!" Bailey declared. "We could do it today, even, and start out your campaign right. We can have a car wash!"

"A car wash?" Maddox said.

"Yeah, for a fundraiser, and like to raise visibility and stuff. My school does them all the time for athletic trips and things like that. All you need is some buckets and rags and things, and you can meet people too, and get the word out." Bailey clapped her hands. "It's perfect! Can we do a car wash today, Aunt Verity?"

"Er ..." Everything seemed to be moving so fast all of a sudden. "Only if Maddox wants to."

"You think it'd be a good idea?" Maddox asked.

He seemed to be asking her. *No worse an idea than any of the rest of it* didn't seem particularly tactful—but the more she thought about it, the more she thought Maddox was right, damn it: someone had to stand up to Hawkins and Ducker, or they'd just keep pushing and pushing, hurting people and destroying this town. They needed supporters; they needed people behind them. One person, alone, couldn't take on Ducker. He kept knocking people down as fast as they tried to go up against him. But there was protection in numbers. This town had needed someone to rally behind. Maybe Maddox was that person.

And they had to start somewhere.

"I think it sounds like a great idea," she said, and Bailey cheered.

MADDOX

They set up the car wash that afternoon in the parking lot of the Whistlestop, after Verity asked permission from the owners. Maddox was amazed at how quickly Bailey had pulled this together. She'd talked to her friends and gotten some supplies from Verity's garden shed, and before he knew it, there he was, with a bunch of high school kids cheerfully throwing sponges at each other, while Bailey and a couple of her friends were sitting with markers making a gigantic sign that read "MADDOX FOR SHERIFF! CLEANING UP THIS TOWN - ONE CAR AT A TIME!"

"It should actually be Murphy," Maddox said, looking over their shoulders. "Maddox is my first name."

"Oh, well, putting your first name on the sign will just make you seem friendlier," was Bailey's reply.

Maddox went over to where Verity was helping some of the kids tie balloons to the Whistlestop's sign. "Hey there," he said to alert her to his presence. "This thing's coming together awfully fast, huh?"

Verity smiled. She looked like she was enjoying herself.

She'd braided up her hair in two plaits wrapped around her head, and she was grinning and, in that moment, was the most beautiful thing he'd ever seen.

My mate. He still couldn't believe it.

And he hated the idea that he might be about to get her in trouble.

"Stop fretting," Verity said, reaching out to grip his arm. "I know what you're thinking. Don't. This thing with Ducker and Hawkins is something we've been ignoring in this town for far too long. It's about time someone put it right out in front of everybody, where they can't ignore it."

"I'm worried that I might make you a target."

"And *I'm* confident that you can protect me." She squeezed his arm again, her hand warm. He wanted to take her in his arms and never let go.

"Maybe Bailey could go sleep at her boyfriend's place for a few nights or something?" Maddox suggested, glancing over at the teenager, who was now directing some of her friends at hanging up the sign. "I mean, not to get rid of her, but ..."

"Oh. Hmm. That *is* a good idea. I wouldn't mind having her out of sight for a bit, in case anything does blow back onto us from this."

It was a gorgeous day, cooler than yesterday, but still warm enough that it wasn't unpleasant to get a little bit wet. On a sunny Saturday afternoon, most of the town seemed to be out and about, and it didn't take long before their car wash was getting a steady stream of customers. The kids were kept busy scrubbing road dust off a string of farm trucks, SUVs, and commuter vehicles. At first, Maddox was almost too shy to talk to people, especially when he saw them staring at his tattoos, but the ice broke when a tiny, white-haired old lady got out of her car and marched up to him.

She looked him up and down. "So," she said. "You're running against that Ted Hawkins, are you?"

"Yes, ma'am," Maddox said, trying to look as nonthreatening as possible.

"Good for you, young man." She put out a thin, shaking hand, as fragile-looking as a sparrow's wing, and he shook it carefully. "It's about time someone put that massive bully in his place. Good luck to you, sir."

She stopped on her way back to her car and thrust a twenty into the jar with the sign reading "CAR WASH FREE - DONATIONS WELCOME!"

After that, people were a lot friendlier, and Maddox got well-wishes and introductions and more dollars shoved into the tip jar. A short, balding man showed up with a camera and asked him a few questions; Maddox only learned after the man hopped back in his now sparkling-clean Volkswagen and puttered off that that had been the lone reporter, editor, and owner of the town's small weekly newspaper.

It was something Maddox had never experienced before, all these people stopping to talk to *him*, and tell him they thought he was doing a good thing, looking at him like he was some kind of hero.

I could get used to this.

But then he looked over at the cane, leaning up against the table where they were keeping the money jar. He had that and the ache in his hip and ankle to remind him of what had happened the last couple of times he decided to play hero.

And then the sheriff's car turned into the parking lot. There was a single whoop of the siren and a flash of the lights before the car stopped and the sheriff got out. He hitched up his belt, looked over the operation, and strolled over. His look at Maddox was long and lingering, and not at all friendly.

"What do you folks think you're doing here?"

"Having a car wash," Verity said, her arms folded.

"You got a permit for that?"

"We don't need a—" Bailey began. Verity hushed her and stepped in front of the kids. Maddox stepped up as well, interposing himself between Verity and the sheriff to loom threateningly.

"Like the lady was saying," Maddox said, "we ain't doing anything we ain't got a perfect right to do. Got permission from the owners and everything." He winced inwardly; when he was stressed, he always found himself lapsing back into talking the way he'd grown up with. It wasn't the best thing when he was trying to make a good impression on authority figures.

"Uh-huh." The sheriff looked up at the sign, fluttering in the wind, at the balloons and the customers nervously pulling away in their half-washed cars. Then he pulled out a ticket book. "I'm going to write you a citation for obstructing traffic and causing a public hazard."

"We were doing nothing of the sort!" Verity snapped, trying to get around Maddox. He quietly moved to keep himself between her and the sheriff, though he was starting to think the issue wasn't so much protecting her *from* the sheriff as protecting her from assaulting-a-police-officer charges if she decided to attack.

"You're in charge here, are you?" the sheriff said, scribbling on his pad.

Verity made a noise like an angry cat.

"The person in charge is me," Maddox said calmly, getting himself between her and the sheriff again. "Anyone gets a ticket here, it oughta be me."

"Oh, don't worry, you will." The sheriff flipped to a new page on his citation book and glanced up at the sign again, then gave Maddox a long, cold look. "What's your last name, then."

"Murphy," Maddox said, and he turned to murmur to Verity, "Hey, you wanna maybe see about getting the kids out of here?"

"Yes. Yes, of course." Verity turned to the teenagers. "I think we're breaking up for now," she said, putting a visibly strained smile on her face. "Each of you can take a little money from the jar to compensate you for your time this afternoon. Bailey, would you go start packing up the hoses?"

Bailey nodded wordlessly, picking up on the tension in the air. Verity squeezed Maddox's arm and then, to his vast relief, went with the teen as they quietly herded the other kids away from the sheriff to start packing up the rags and buckets. Hawkins barely glanced after them, paying little attention, before turning his glare back to Maddox. Clearly the others were beneath his notice. *And let's hope they stay that way.*

"*I'm* the only candidate for sheriff this election cycle," Hawkins said. "Deadline was yesterday."

"Yeah, and I got my paperwork in," Maddox said. "Got a packet of stuff this morning and everything. It's official."

"Then you'll be dropping out."

"Nope." Maddox crossed his arms. "Not gonna happen."

The sheriff leaned forward. He was actually a little shorter than Maddox, which became apparent when they went nose to nose. Maddox could see a look of slight apprehension cross the sheriff's face as he apparently realized that he was at a physical disadvantage here. He was a big guy and probably was used to pushing around whoever he wanted.

Yeah, you try pushing around a bull, buddy. We don't budge.

The sheriff settled his hand on the butt of his service weapon and seemed to use that for renewed courage. "So you got away the other night," he murmured in Maddox's face. "You got lucky. Think you could be that lucky twice?"

"Seems like the way I remember it, you *lost* the other

night," Maddox muttered back. "Couldn't win a fight with me 'til you brought a Ford for backup. You wanna go again? How lucky you think you'll get this time?"

The sheriff sucked in a breath, puffing out his chest, and Maddox curled his hands into fists. If the guy wanted to go right here in the parking lot in front of a dozen witnesses, Maddox was willing to do it.

But they were interrupted by the rumble of an engine, and Ducker's big, gleaming black truck pulled into the parking lot. Maddox had only seen it in the dusk last night, and it was even more impressive by daylight, freshly washed without a speck of dust on it (*What does he do, go through the car wash every day?* Maddox thought), with a gleaming chrome grille and a lift kit and a rack of lights above the cab.

"Saved by the bell, huh?" Maddox murmured as the sheriff took a step back, taking his hand off his weapon.

Ducker stepped down from the truck's cab, dapper and silver-haired. When he approached, Maddox could see the swelling of a bruise still visible on his jaw. It had been expertly covered with pancake makeup to conceal the colors, but it was there.

"What's going on here, exactly?" Ducker inquired.

"Your pet sheriff's throwing his weight around," Maddox said before Hawkins could say anything. "Lucky for him Daddy showed up before he got his ass handed to him, again."

"You know what? I think a night in jail would cool you off *real* nice," the sheriff snarled. He drew his gun half out of the holster.

"Quiet down, Ted," Ducker said, holding out a hand. For a tense moment, the sheriff didn't move; then, slowly, he slid the gun back into place.

"Daddy said no," Maddox murmured. The sheriff's face turned purple.

"It might be in your best interests, son, to stop antago-nizing the local power structure," Ducker said pleasantly. He looked up at the sign that Bailey and Verity were taking down. "Running for sheriff, are you? You do have a set of balls on you, don't you, boy." For the first time the pleasant veneer slipped somewhat, and Maddox glimpsed the snake-like coldness underneath the genial surface.

"Not just running," Maddox said. "I plan to win."

"Do you, now."

"Why are we putting up with this?" the sheriff demanded in an undertone. "I'll just run him in to the station ... and maybe he'll have a little accident along the way."

"You ever think about putting a leash on your dog?" Maddox wanted to know.

"You son of a bitch, I'm going to—"

"I said calm down, Ted." This time there was a snap of command in Ducker's voice. The sheriff subsided, breathing heavily, and Ducker gestured to the café. "Why don't we go have a cup of coffee and talk this over like civilized people."

Maddox had to stop himself from looking Verity's way. The less Ducker and Hawkins knew about how close they were, the better. He could only hope she wouldn't try to come in after him. "Yeah," he said. "Cup of coffee'd be great."

They slid into a booth at the Whistlestop. Ducker sat across from Maddox, and the sheriff pulled up a chair on the outside of the booth, half blocking the aisle (to the waitress's visible annoyance) and stopping Maddox from being able to easily leave. Maddox could have smiled; how many times had he pulled the same trick himself?

He wasn't afraid of Ducker, not in a public place like this.

Men like Ducker weren't so dangerous in public. It was afterwards, in the dark, that the knives came out.

"I don't know if you're the bravest man I've met, or simply the stupidest," Ducker remarked, sipping at a cup of coffee. "Most men would have left town after what happened to you the other day."

"I'm not the running kind," Maddox said.

"You're gonna learn," Hawkins said darkly.

Ducker gave him a quelling look, and the sheriff shut up. "Let's not be uncivilized about this. I think what we have here is a difference of opinion that ought to be relatively easy to resolve. So your name is Maddox Murphy, is it? Friends call you Maddox?"

"You're not my friend."

"Oh, but I'd like to be ... Maddox. You know, this county is very happy with Ted here as their sheriff."

"Funny," Maddox said. "That's not what I've heard from the actual people in this town."

"Oh, really? You've been in town for, what, two days, and you're suddenly an expert on what people in this town want and need?"

"I know what they don't need, and that's a small-time bully like *Ted* here." Maddox glanced at him, and found the sheriff glaring at him with undisguised loathing. "Trust me, I know his type."

"*Do* you now," Ducker said quietly. "What exactly is your experience in this area, Maddox?"

"None of your damn business, is what it is," Maddox said, and knew he'd made a mistake when a flicker of cool satisfaction crossed Ducker's face.

"Oh? You know something, Maddox. I expect you have talents in the same areas Ted does. Useful talents. I expect, in fact, that I might have a lot of use for a man like you."

"*What?*" The sheriff gave him a shocked look. "You can't possibly—"

"I didn't ask you, Ted. I'm speaking to Mr. Murphy here. And what I'd like very much to know, *Maddox*, is whether you might be interested in a job."

Maddox made himself smile, although he didn't want to. It was a smile he'd practiced on some of his previous jobs. A scary smile. "You remember I flattened you the other day, right? You sure you want me around?"

Ducker's face went cool and still. His eyes were cold as ice. "I'll be honest here. What I *want* is to turn Ted loose on you and stand back and enjoy it as he beats you to a pulp. But I'm a practical man. I haven't gotten where I am today by letting go of a useful asset."

"Yeah," Maddox said quietly. "That's what people are to men like you, right? *Assets*. No thanks. I'm not interested in your job offer."

"I'd take some time to think about it, if I were you. This is an offer you don't want to turn down."

"I don't need time to think. I'd rather shovel cowshit than take a single dollar from you. In fact, sir, that's an insult to cowshit. Shoveling shit is a good honest occupation, unlike working for you."

Ducker's face had gone colder and colder with every word. "Son, you want to take some advice from me—"

"Oh, and that's the other thing," Maddox said. This felt so freeing, all of a sudden. It was like being able to go back to all the terrible mafia bosses he'd ever worked for, everyone who'd helped shape him into a person he hated being, and give a big middle finger to all of them. "I'm not your son. I'm not your boy. I'm not your friend. I don't take advice from you, I'm never going to work for you, and ..." He shoved the cup of cooling coffee away from him, not without a little regret since coffee was in short supply around Verity's house. "I don't even want your stupid coffee."

He got up. The sheriff got up too. For a long moment they just stared at each other. Maddox threw back his shoulders to make himself look bigger than he was, emphasizing how his muscles strained against his T-shirt; it was a trick he'd used in the past, one he wasn't proud of, but it was often effective. The sheriff showed no signs of backing down; he'd dropped his hand to the butt of his service weapon again.

"Not here, Ted," Ducker said quietly. There wasn't a hint of friendliness anymore in his face or tone.

The sheriff hesitated just long enough to make Maddox wonder if this was going to be the time when the dog slipped his leash. Then he stepped out of the way, enough to give Maddox room to get out of the booth (barely), though Maddox still had to push past him to get out.

Maddox walked out of the restaurant, feeling their eyes on him and trying his damnedest not to limp. It was like being surrounded by wolves or sharks: you didn't want to show weakness.

In the parking lot, the kids were nowhere in sight and everything had been packed up and vanished along with the teens and their farm trucks. All that was left were Verity and Bailey, sitting on the curb waiting for him. He wished they hadn't; in fact, he almost walked by them without saying anything, because the absolute last thing he wanted was for the sheriff and Ducker (who he *knew* were watching out the window) to see them greet him. But Bailey was already jumping to her feet, holding out his cane.

Maddox reluctantly took it. "Hey," he said, as Verity hooked her arm through his. "You know what we talked about, with Bailey going to her boyfriend's place? I think she oughta do that. And we need to get out of here."

"Wait, I'm doing what now?" Bailey protested, as they

started walking. Maddox forced himself not to look over his shoulder. It was a short walk back to Verity and Bailey's place, all of it on very public streets, and it was the middle of the day. They didn't have anything to worry about. Yet.

"You're going to pack an overnight bag when we get home and go over to Luke's grandma's place," Verity said firmly.

"Think she'll be safe there?" Maddox asked.

"I know she will. Luke lives on the rez—the Indian reservation. The sheriff has no jurisdiction there, and Ducker knows he's not welcome."

"You should go too."

Verity shook her head.

"What's going on?" Bailey asked. "Are you guys in trouble?"

"Bullies don't like it when people stand up to them," Maddox said. "Sometimes they do dumb things. Verity, I'm goddamn sorry I got you into this."

Verity pressed his arm. "You didn't get me into anything. You were right all along. We can't just sit around and let Ducker and his pet sheriff squeeze the lifeblood out of this town. Someone had to stand up to him eventually. It might as well be us."

VERITY

I t surprised Verity a little that she wasn't more afraid
than she was. But she'd meant what she said to
Maddox. She was *glad* someone had finally decided to
stand up to Ducker and Hawkins. She just hoped too much
of the blowback didn't fall on Bailey.

After some arguing, Bailey had finally agreed to pack up
and go stay with Luke's family. One of Luke's uncles swung
by in a farm truck to pick her up, and Verity finally breathed
a long sigh of relief as the truck rattled off into the distance.

"Still wish I could get you to go with her," Maddox said,
his voice heavy.

"I'm not going to run," Verity said. "It's my town. My
problem."

"Our problem."

She reached out and his hand settled in hers. Verity
squeezed his fingers. "Our problem."

She intended to leave the store locked up for the rest of
the day, but then the doorbell rang, and there was a constant
stream of visitors who had either heard about the confronta-
tion in the parking lot or had picked up the Saturday-after-

noon weekly paper and had found out about Maddox's candidacy. Everyone wanted to shake his hand. Eventually Verity flipped the sign back to CLOSED and locked up the shop just to give them some peace.

"This whole town has been waiting for someone like you to show up," she told Maddox while she puttered around in the kitchen, making them a early dinner.

"I'm not a leader," Maddox said, sounding uncomfortable.

"What we need isn't a leader, not really. We can handle that part for ourselves. What we need is someone to give us hope."

"Never thought I'd be that, either."

He sounded so depressed, so downcast. Verity turned away from the sink. "Maddox," she began, and then stopped.

They'd never talked about his past, not even once. She had no idea what had led him to wander into their town, apparently without a single attachment in the world. But now, when she *could* have asked, she caught herself and stopped.

Because it really didn't matter to her. Wherever he'd been, whoever he'd been, she didn't care. She knew who he was now, and that was the important thing.

And maybe he needed to hear that.

"You are now," she said simply. "We needed hope. You brought us that. Now it's out there in the town, and it's spreading. I think Hawkins and Ducker aren't going to find us nearly as easy to push around anymore."

"You might be surprised," Maddox said gloomily. "I shouldn't have pushed so hard, so fast. When you push bullies, they push back. I made 'em back down in front of the whole town. Now they're gonna want to make an example out of me. That's how it works. I don't care so much if they come after me, but what I don't like is the idea they might come after you."

"They've come after me before, remember? I got through it all right. And now I have you to protect me."

"I just hope things don't end up worse for you than if I'd never come here."

"They won't." She found his shoulder with a light touch, and used that to guide herself into his lap, straddling his legs. "I'm glad you're here. I'm looking forward to facing whatever comes next—together."

His lips found hers, and their gentle kiss turned heated.

"You know," Verity murmured, "we have a whole evening in front of us without a teenager in the house. I can turn off the stove under that taco meat and we can have a little pre-dinner appetizer, if you feel like it."

They made love and then ate a leisurely dinner of burritos and salad, sitting on the balcony with the evening growing cool around them. There was a chill in the air that hadn't been there just a few nights ago.

"So how cold does it get here?" Maddox asked. "Cold enough to snow?"

"Up in the mountains. Not so much down here. Once or twice a winter, maybe."

"I've never really been in the desert much. It's different from what I'm used to."

"This isn't really even desert around here," Verity said. "It's more ranch country. Go south a little ways, and then you'll see *real* desert."

"I'd like to go down there sometime." His hand brushed hers, a kind of feeling-out touch to avoid startling her before taking her hand. She wondered if he knew how much those little courtesies meant to her. "What do you think about a little trip, when we get through all of this?"

"Oh," she said. She and Bailey never really went anywhere; Bailey had just recently gotten her driver's license, and there was exactly one taxicab in the entire town, so Verity usually relied on neighbors to drive her places. Long driving trips were out of the question. Anyway, she'd never really had much desire to travel. It wasn't like she could look at scenery, and she liked knowing where everything was. The idea of finding her way around new places and sitting in a car for hours sounded like the opposite of fun to her.

But then she thought about doing it with Maddox. Sitting in a car no longer sounded like a chore if she had Maddox to talk to. And he could tell her what he was seeing, and show her around new places without making her feel like she was too slow or a burden—or the opposite, with Bailey, where she was the one who was supposed to be in charge, so there was always the pressure on her to make sure that she was never lost or disoriented.

"Do you like traveling?" she asked Maddox.

"I guess I've never really stopped to think if it's something I like or not," he said after a moment. "It's just something I've been doing. I used to go new places for ... work, and then I kinda didn't have anywhere to settle down." He hesitated again. "I think ... I do like seeing new places, but I also have been moving around so much because I've been looking for something, and that something was home." He ran his fingers, rough with calluses, across her smoother ones. "That something was you."

Her heart turned over in her chest. "I think I've been looking for you too, without knowing I was," she said shyly. "I *am* kind of a homebody, I admit it. But I think I might like to go somewhere new, if you were there. If traveling is something you'd like to do."

"I think I might, but I'd want somewhere to come back to."

"You'll always have that." She could feel the smile breaking out on her face, and she hoped he was smiling back. In fact ... there was no reason why she couldn't find out. She reached out and brushed the backs of her fingers across his lips, and yes, there was a smile, along with a scruff of beard stubble.

"Oh, you know what, Maddox, we should see if I have a spare razor in the bathroom. In fact, there are a lot of things you need if you're going to look respectable enough to beat Hawkins and Ducker at their own game. We can do a bit of shopping tomorrow."

"I don't have much money."

"Oh, Maddox, don't worry about it. I expect that once you explain to the business owners in town that you're trying to oust Hawkins, they'll give you whatever you want. Ugh, those bullies. I don't know why we've put up with them for so long."

In the bathroom, she dug out the box of supplies and found the bag of razors that Bailey used to shave her legs. She found a spot among the girly clutter around the sink to lay one out for Maddox.

We're going to need to make space for his things, she thought.

Was this really likely to become that permanent?

Yes. At least, I hope so.

Verity woke with the vague sense that something was wrong.

She lay with her head pillowed on Maddox's chest, listening to his quiet breathing and trying to figure out what had awakened her. She felt dazed and heavy, with sleep trying to drag her back down ... but no, that wasn't right, because she usually woke up feeling bright and active; she was a natural morning person. Then again, she also wasn't a terribly light sleeper, so she rarely woke up at night like this.

She'd been having an unpleasant dream, and maybe that was it. She hated the wildfires that had started becoming more common in the summer, and she'd been dreaming about one of those, a brushfire chasing her through the town. It had been a sort of liquid fire with a texture like egg yolk, not really burning things, not even burning her when she touched it, but leaping in its weird fluid way from one house to another, and always finding her when she tried to hide. Now she was left with the unsettled feeling that always went along with waking up from a bad dream.

She could also still smell the smoke from the dream, which was contributing to the uneasy feeling.

Actually ...

Actually, that really *was* smoke.

Verity sat bolt upright in bed and shook Maddox. "Wake up! Maddox, something's on fire."

Stupid, she thought, scrambling for her robe as Maddox began to stir. Stupid, to think Hawkins and Ducker wouldn't try something different this time. She'd thought at worst they might vandalize the shop again, or send some thugs—or the sheriff himself—to try the same kind of intimidation tactics they'd tried before.

Stupid, stupid, stupid.

When she opened the door into the hall, the acrid wildfire smell was much stronger. *Thank God* that Bailey was over at Luke's—and also that Maddox was here, because he could tell her where the smoke was coming from, without her having to try to follow her nose to the source of it.

"Do you see the fire?" she asked, stumbling into the kitchen, and then she stopped because she'd left her phone in the bedroom.

"I don't think it's upstairs. I think it's below us."

"The shop. Damn it." She tried to push past Maddox, back into the bedroom. He caught her.

"What are you doing? You need to get out."

"I need to get my phone and call the fire department."

"You need to get *out*. Get downstairs. I'll get your phone."

"But I know exactly where it is." She gave him a little shake, hands gripped onto his arms. "Maddox, there's no time to argue. Go downstairs and find out where the fire is. I'll be down in a minute."

She knew he wasn't happy, but he let go of her arms and she plunged into the hallway. Her phone was where she always kept it at night, plugged in on her nightstand. "Nine-one-one," she told it, as she started to run back into the hall, then stopped for her slippers, since she was here anyway. Oh, and her wallet—damn it! Maddox was right though, she had to stop grabbing things and get out.

Stuffing her wallet into a pocket of her robe while giving hurried instructions to the dispatch operator on the phone, she hurried down the back stairs. The back door of the shop stood open and she heard banging sounds coming from inside.

"Maddox?" she shouted, and then started coughing as she stepped inside. The smoke was much denser inside the shop.

"It's on the porch," he shouted back. "You have a hose in the garden, right?"

"Yes, I'll get it."

She ran to the hose rack and unwound it around the side of the house. "Maddox?" she called, and heard him jump off the porch. His big hands took the hose from hers. "How bad it is?"

"Bad, but I think we caught it in time. You call for help?"

"I did," she said, and just then her elderly neighbor's voice shouted across the fence, "Verity? What's happening over there?"

"Betty! We have a fire over here!"

"Just a minute, I'll wake up Ed!" the old lady's voice came back.

There were sirens now. The volunteer fire department was just down the street, so she expected a quick response. But already pounding feet on the sidewalk let her know that more of her neighbors had arrived, and now there were shouts of, "I'll bring the hose around from our garden," and "Ed, hand me that shovel!"

Verity found herself pushed to the side. Her first reaction was incredible frustration. But she really couldn't do much without getting underfoot. She took a breath of the now somewhat cleaner air. *What* can *I do?* She could bring tools, she thought, and hurried back around the side of the house to gather what she had in the garden shed.

By the time she came back, the fire trucks were drawing up outside in a squeal of sirens. Verity considered going upstairs to rescue some of her things, but instead decided to simply to stay out of the way. Something brushed her shoulder, startling her, and then Maddox's hand slipped into hers. With all the noise and commotion and smoke smells covering up the usual cues she relied on, it was harder to recognize individuals.

"Is it out?" she asked.

"Think so. Looks like it's down to the fire department cleaning up the hot spots." His voice was raspy. Her throat ached too, seared raw by the smoke—and by worry and grief for the business she'd spent her adult life building.

"How bad ..." The question caught in her sore throat before she could quite finish it.

"Not too much damage," Maddox said, and she felt like she could breathe again. "It looks like they threw a bunch of diesel-soaked rags on the porch. Luckily they're really bad at this. First of all, diesel doesn't burn worth a damn compared to gasoline, and you want to start a fire properly, you'd put 'em under the porch where they're hard to get at, or throw something through the window—"

"Maddox," she said. Her voice cracked again. "I don't think this is the time."

"Sorry." It came out very contrite. He put an arm around her.

"I'm sorry too. Maddox, if we'd slept through it, we might have both been killed."

"And I'm the one they're after." It came out a growl, like an angry animal noise.

"Not your fault." She leaned into him. "Just ... hold me for a minute."

When she felt a little steadier, she went upstairs to make pitchers of iced tea for the thirsty firefighters, neighbors and fire-truck volunteers alike. She broke out all the packages of tea cookies that she had in the store, and Betty and Ed brought over a bunch of plastic lawn furniture from next door to sit on. There was a friendly air of camaraderie among the whole fire-fighting group; it was easy to forget, almost, the reek of smoke in the air and the fact that she was in her bathrobe and it was still the middle of the night.

The party atmosphere prevailed until Maddox stood up suddenly, almost upsetting Verity's plastic cup of ice tea. "Look who's here," he said, his voice dropping to that rumbling, growl-like register.

"Well, look at this. Sheriff Hawkins," Betty said, before Verity could ask who it was. Tires crunched by the curb. "A day late and a dollar short, so help me." The old woman's tone was scathing. No one had suggested calling the police about the fire; they'd all had enough problems with Hawkins that every last one of them knew who was probably responsible.

The door of the police cruiser slammed and Hawkins'

heavy tread crunched on the sidewalk. "Well, that's a terrible thing there, Miss Breslin," he said to Verity. "Terrible thing."

"Yes," Verity said politely, standing up and keeping a firm grip on her temper. "It *is* a terrible thing. Do you plan to do anything about investigating it?"

"Law and order in this town is something I take very seriously," the sheriff said.

There were a couple of snorts and scoffing sounds from the assembled neighbors. Everyone was feeling bolder already, Verity realized. No one wanted to stand up to the sheriff if they were the only one, but the feeling of unity was beginning to spread.

"And where were you, Mr. Murphy, when this fire was set?" the sheriff asked, and Verity's indignant anger suddenly had a new source.

"He was with me!" she snapped.

"A likely story. A drifter from out of town, hanging around the site of a criminal act of arson? Seems suspicious to me. Come on, son, let's take a ride down to the station."

There was a sudden scuffling next to her. "No!" Verity cried, reaching out in the sheriff's direction. Hard hands smacked hers away, and there was a meaty sound of a fist striking flesh—she wasn't sure whose—and a gasp and a tiny cheer from somewhere in the crowd.

"That's assaulting an officer," Hawkins choked out. "You're going in for arson and assault, Murphy, and if you don't come with me this minute, I'm getting every deputy who's on duty tonight and running in this entire crowd for disturbing the peace. And *she's* coming with you as an accomplice. We'll see how you both like cooling your heels in jail."

"Maddox, don't!" Verity said, because all sounds of resistance had stopped, and the crowd was dead silent. In that silence, there was a loud clicking sound that she didn't recognize at first, not until she reached out for

Maddox and felt the cold steel of handcuffs on his wrists. "Maddox, no! Sheriff, he didn't do it. He was with me. The entire place would have burned if he hadn't helped put it out!"

"You going in easy, or do I have to take her too?" the sheriff said, his voice low and threatening.

"It's okay, Verity," Maddox said. "If I'm not here, you won't be in danger. Just let me go with him."

"Maddox, no!" She clung to him as the sheriff marched him across the sidewalk, trying to hang back and getting halfway dragged. "He tried to kill you once, don't you remember that? Every single one of you needs to know this. Sheriff Hawkins tried to kill this man, and he's going to try to kill him again, and I'm *not* letting you take him!"

"Verity, don't." Maddox's hands were cuffed, but he turned his body to hip-check her away from the sheriff. "You're safer without me—"

"Bullshit!" She almost never cursed, but this was the sort of situation that called for it. "We're in this together!"

"—And there's nothing you can do if you're locked up next to me," Maddox went on, and his words were like a bucket of ice water dashed over her flaming anger. He was right; out of jail, with her entire network of friends and neighbors plus the internet to lean on, she could get help for him, get him a lawyer, rally the townsfolk.

None of which would do him any good if Sheriff Hawkins planned to take him out in the desert and shoot him.

But it wasn't like she could do more to help if she was in danger right along with him.

"Okay," she said, and her hand trailed off his arm as he was manhandled out of her reach—and, effectively, out of her world, a world that largely stopped at the ends of her fingertips. "You better treat him well, Ted Hawkins, or I'm going to find the biggest, meanest law firm in this corner of the state and unleash them on you."

"Yeah, whatever," the sheriff grunted. "Into the car, Murphy."

"Verity?" Maddox's voice was slightly muffled now. "I love you."

No man had ever said that to her before. The words struck her with such force that all she could do was stand there, hand upraised and every possible reply dying in her throat. It was only as the cruiser's engine revved and the tires crunched that it really sank in that she hadn't said it back and she might never see him again.

She stood there in her bathrobe and, for a terrible minute, felt utterly bereft, entirely desolate.

And then she turned to the people around her, who she knew were still there by their little rustles and an occasional awkward cough.

"So you all just stood there and let Ted Hawkins take him," she said bitterly.

A cold, thin hand patted her arm, and Betty said, "Verity, dear, what could we do? He's the *sheriff*."

Verity turned away, clenching her fists. "I understand you're afraid," she said. "I'm afraid too. But don't you see? The way they win is by dividing us. Together, we're stronger than they are. And they *know* that. Keeping us scared and separated is what they count on."

No one spoke, and she was suddenly very tired. It wasn't fair to blame them. They were just ordinary people trying to live their lives. No one wanted to get on the bad side of people like Hawkins and Ducker. Everyone else had families and jobs to worry about, too.

It was just that she was so terribly, terribly afraid for Maddox.

If he doesn't come back, I'm going to find a way to bring both of you down. No matter what.

There was still an awkward silence around her. Verity carefully tucked away her anger into a deep dark corner of her soul; there would be time for anger later, but now was the time for bridge-building, for reminding these people that they were all on the same side. "If I could get some help carrying the tea cups upstairs and packing up my hose and tools," she said, "I think I have more cookies if anyone wants some."

She didn't think that it was her imagination that there seemed to be relief in the sudden flurry of activity around her. These were good people, just scared. They wanted to do the right thing; they just didn't want to jeopardize their homes and families by doing it.

But someone had to be the one to step up. Someone had to set an example for everyone else to follow. Maddox had been that person, and now she knew it was her turn to step forward and do it herself.

In the morning, she had every intention of paying a visit to the sheriff's department, armed with the phone numbers of the best lawyers she could find.

And Maddox had better be there, safe and sound, or there would be hell to pay.

MADDOX

As the sheriff's cruiser pulled away, Maddox twisted around to look back at Verity standing at the curb. She wouldn't be looking after him, of course—there was no reason for her to ... but she was, face turned in his direction, standing small and defiant in front of her fire-scorched business. He lost sight of her only when the cruiser turned the corner. In his last glimpse of her, she was still looking his way.

"You sure are getting yourself in a heap of trouble for only having been in town for a couple of days," the sheriff said from the front seat.

"Yeah, and whose fault is that?" Maddox tested his cuffs, wondering if he could use shifter strength to break them. He didn't think so, at least not without hurting his wrists. And he couldn't shift with his arms twisted behind his back like this; it would break his bull's shoulders.

The sheriff gave a snort, sounding a lot like a bull himself.

They weren't driving into town, where Maddox would have expected the sheriff's department to be. Instead they were heading out toward the highway. He felt a clutch of something that wasn't precisely fear, more like a kind of tense excitement. "Are you actually gonna take me out in the desert and shoot me, after you arrested me in front of a couple dozen witnesses?"

The sheriff snorted again. "We're just gonna have a little talk, you and me. *Just* you and me this time. No interfering busybodies to stop me from doing my job."

"Yeah, that Ducker guy must be passing you some fat envelopes full of cash to yank you around like he does. Or are you banging his wife, or what?"

"You can just shut up back there."

Maddox tested the cuffs again. He felt like the left might be a little looser than the right. All he had to do was get one of them off.

And maybe get a little of your cooperation this time, he thought at his bull.

His bull had been a lot more present in his head since he'd met Verity, but there was still the barrier between them that had been there ever since he'd been hurt, the bull's evident reluctance to come out and shift.

What is your problem, anyway? Maddox thought at his inner animal. *Do you hate me that much, or what? You better get over it, 'cause I think if you don't, we're both getting a bullet in the head.*

I don't hate you, his bull answered. *I'm ... ashamed.*

You're what?

The answer came reluctantly, from the deepest part of his soul. *All our lives we've relied on my strength. But when you really needed me, it wasn't enough.*

What the hell, you dumbass ox? That's what it's been all this time? We had a building collapse on us and then we had to fight a bunch of giant stone statues come to life. Of course we weren't going to win. We held 'em off long enough for Darius and his lady to get away. That's all we had to do.

His bull hesitated; he could feel that it was thinking about what to say but couldn't decide. He'd never felt this kind of uncertainty from his animal. Usually it knew exactly what it wanted, charging into things exactly like the bull it was.

Except ... it had been this way ever since he'd been hurt, hadn't it? He had mistaken its hesitation for anger, because that was the feeling he was mainly used to from that part of his soul. His bull was his fierce side, his confidence, his willingness to throw himself into a fight.

And then they'd been wounded—*he'd* been wounded, body and soul. His body had never recovered fully. Even now, his hip ached, a sharp reminder that without his cane (or even with it), he wasn't going to be able to outrun Hawkins in the desert night.

Was it any surprise that his soul hadn't recovered either?

His first instinct was to get angry at himself. But he'd gone through that during his recovery, nursing a bottomless frustration with his body's weakness. It had only pushed him and his bull farther apart.

Instead he tried to think what he might say to Verity or to Bailey, if they were upset and feeling inadequate and hurt. He wouldn't want to yell at them, but he also wouldn't want to soothe them with pretty, meaningless lies. And lying to yourself never ended well, anyway.

Listen, we went through a really bad thing, he thought to that wounded corner of his soul. *We're never going to be the same as we were before. But that's okay. We don't think Verity's weak or a bad person because she can't see, right?*

A surge of appalled rage came from his bull at the very idea. Verity was beautiful and perfect and strong and capable and—

Yeah, I get it, I agree. So let's ease up on ourselves a little bit, too. We aren't perfect, and we aren't quite what we used to be. But we did our best, getting here.

We lost a fight, his bull grumbled. *We lost THE fight, the biggest fight of our lives.*

Yeah, I know. But for awhile there, we really gave those monsters a fight, didn't we? We kicked some stony ass.

His bull huffed in satisfaction, and the memories dropped into his head: not the ones he'd dwelled on for all these months, the crunch of his shattered hip and the agony of trying to walk on a broken leg—but, instead, the satisfying impact of his hooves meeting stony flesh, the glee of watching those fierce stone constructs scatter in front of his charge.

We gave 'em a good fight, his bull agreed.

Yeah, we did. So you want to come out here and help me give this puffed-up bully a run for his money too?

Wordless agreement came from that fierce corner of his soul, along with a swell of confidence. And Maddox grinned quietly to himself in the dark backseat.

They were a ways out of town now, with nothing on either side of the patrol cruiser except endless darkness. They'd left the highway behind, and the seat jolted under him as they navigated over rocks and washouts.

Yeah, Maddox thought. "Talk" or not, you didn't take someone way out in the desert like this for good reasons.

The sheriff stopped the car and opened the driver's door, leaving the engine running. Maddox twisted his wrist in the left-hand cuff, scraping the skin until he felt the stickiness of blood. The pain barely registered. It didn't matter; he was settling into that calm, tense, slightly high state that came before a fight.

The sheriff wrenched open the back door. "Get out."

Maddox obeyed.

It hadn't felt cold in town, but out here in the desert, there was a sharp chill in the air. They were down in some kind of gully. The cruiser's headlights lit up tangled snarls of dead-looking brush and a plain of ancient water-washed rocks, jagged and dark and dry, stretching out to the edge of the pool of light.

"You gonna kill me?" Maddox asked. He wasn't afraid at all. Instead he was perfectly centered, at one with his bull at last. Its confidence—*his* confidence—lifted him up and straightened his spine.

"I haven't decided yet," the sheriff said. "Walk."

They walked away from the cruiser, into the brush and rocks, until the rumble of the engine faded behind them. A nearly full moon lit up the desert like wan daylight punctuated with stark black shadows. The sky was perfectly clear overhead, the stars so sharp and bright it seemed to Maddox that he could reach out and touch them.

He was intensely aware of every sound the sheriff made, the crunch of boots behind him. When Maddox stopped abruptly and turned around, the sheriff took a step back, and drew his gun halfway out of the holster.

"What's in this for you, anyway?" Maddox asked. "What do you get out of being Ducker's attack dog?"

The sheriff drew the weapon the rest of the way. "You better stop calling me that."

"Listen, I've been where you are. I used to let rich bastards like him pay me to do their dirty work too. There's no pension in a job like that, know what I mean?" Maddox stiffly stuck out his gimp leg. "If you're lucky, you end up like me— broke, half crippled, and hitchhiking from one little town to another, with nobody in the world who cares about me. And that's one of the *good* outcomes."

"Shut up," Hawkins said, but he hadn't shot him yet, so at least he was listening.

"Is it just about the money? He got some kind of dirt on you?"

"I said shut up."

"Because if it's the money, trust me, you can make money some other way. Maybe you won't make the kind of money that men like Ducker pay for loyalty, but that kind of money doesn't just come with strings attached, it comes with industrial-sized steel cables." Maddox risked taking his eyes off the sheriff for a moment to flick a glance at the rocky wilderness around them. "You ever think, when you first put on that uniform and that badge, that you'd end up doing the kind of things you do for him? Is this what you wanted—to end up *here*?"

"You don't know what you're talking about."

The gun didn't waver. Maddox hadn't thought he'd be able to successfully talk Hawkins around to his side, but while he was talking, he'd been quietly working his left hand out of the cuff, hidden behind his back. Now he gave it a terrific wrench and pulled it out, raking the skin from his wrist all the way down to the fingers. He was gonna be feeling *that* when the adrenaline wore off. But at least his hands were free, the cuffs rattling loosely from his right wrist.

The sheriff squeezed the trigger, but it was a reflexive jerk, more of an instinctive reaction than an actual attempt to kill him, and Maddox was already flinging himself to the side. The shot hit the ground and kicked up dust and rock chips, while Maddox rolled into the brush.

The sheriff cursed. Maddox picked himself up on his hands and knees. Hawkins was turning wildly around, the gun held out in front of him. The moonlight was bright enough to see by, dimly but Maddox was now cloaked in ink-black shadows.

This would be the perfect opportunity to get out of here. Maddox was pretty sure he could make a run for the cruiser in his bull form (he still had three good legs, after all) and leave the sheriff to make his own way back out of the desert.

But that wouldn't solve anything; it would just mean that he'd have an even more pissed-off sheriff to deal with.

No. He wouldn't run. This had to be dealt with here, just the two of them.

The sheriff seemed to have realized the vulnerability of the cruiser as a getaway vehicle, and he was backing toward it. Letting him get all the way to the car would be a mistake.

Maddox lunged to his feet and shifted.

It felt *good*. It was like two pieces of a puzzle coming together, like the broken pieces of himself suddenly fitting into a new, whole shape. He didn't feel damaged anymore, despite the deformity of the hip that was never going to heal right. He felt whole, powerful, strong.

Maddox's bull was no ordinary Black Angus. No fence had ever contained a bull like this, enormous and shaggy, kin to the ancestral wild aurochs that had been painted on cave walls, from which all domestic cattle came.

He charged out of the brush, out of the darkness and the night, the empty handcuff rattling above his hoof.

The sheriff yelled in startled terror and snapped off a wild shot; Maddox felt it burn across his shoulder. He veered just enough to clip Hawkins with his shoulder rather than trampling him. Even a glancing blow from a bull this size would have felt like getting slapped with a concrete wall. Hawkins went down hard, all the breath huffing out of him, and the gun flew out of his hand. Maddox dug in his hooves for a sharp turn. As Hawkins, gasping, struggled to reach the gun, Maddox kicked it away from him into the brush. Then he planted one enormous hoof on the sheriff's rib cage.

He could easily have crushed him, and it was briefly tempting ... but that wasn't who he was now. Not anymore. When the townspeople started looking at him like a hero, they were changing him, though he hadn't even realized it at the time. But now he couldn't bear the idea of not acting like the man they thought he was—the man Verity thought he was.

So he shifted back instead, kneeling and naked with his palm flat on Hawkins' chest. His scraped-raw hand burned and his shoulder stung where the bullet had creased him; he could feel blood trickling down his arm, which didn't improve his mood any.

The sheriff stared at him with eyes as round as saucers. "What ..."

"First of all," Maddox said, "if you tell anyone about this, no one is ever gonna believe you. So just keep that in mind."

"What," the sheriff said again, faintly, and then he lurched upward with a wrestling move intended to throw Maddox off him. Maddox had anticipated this, and he shifted back to his bull. Hawkins found himself slamming into Maddox's massive leg, like ramming a tree trunk, and fell flat on his back again.

Maddox tapped him with a big hoof and then, while the sheriff panted for breath (it would have been like getting punched in the stomach), shifted back again with his hand planted firmly on Hawkins' chest.

"You gonna be reasonable and talk a bit?"

"Huuurrk," was Hawkins' breathless response. Maybe that hoof-tap had been a little firmer than intended.

Maddox waited patiently. When Hawkins could speak again, he gasped out, "What *are* you?"

"Nobody you want to mess with, but I'm thinking you figured that out already." He eased back a little, since Hawkins didn't seem to be trying to get up this time. "So maybe now you'll answer the question I asked earlier. Is it just about the money for you, or is Ducker buying your loyalty some other way?"

Hawkins was quiet for a minute, and then he said heavily, "It's both. The money's good, hell, better than good. Nobody working for a small-town sheriff's department could afford the kind of house I live in, good debt-free college for both our kids, nice vacations for me and the wife twice a year. But ..." He hesitated. Maddox waited. "I had ... problems, when I was a kid. Ran with a bad crowd. Did drugs for awhile. I did ... things I'm not proud of to get money for those drugs. Armed robbery, that kind of thing. I could've gone to prison for a long time.

"I got myself clean, but when it came to the rest of it, Ducker stepped in to help. He made all that go away. I wouldn't be where I am today if not for him."

"Except he could take it away anytime he wanted," Maddox said quietly. He thought about his own ill-spent youth, the things he'd done while working for men just like Ducker—with far less reason than Hawkins had. For him, it really *had* been about the money. Or, rather, it had been that he didn't think he was good enough for better work. When all his job skills consisted of strong-arming shopkeepers for protection money and bodyguarding mobsters, what kind of career was he going to move into, anyway?

"Yeah," Hawkins said softly. "And he never let me forget it. Don't get me wrong, he pays me damn well for what he has me do."

"But you both know who's holding the leash."

Hawkins' face twisted.

"And tonight," Maddox said, with his bull's anger flowing through him, "you set fire to a good woman's business, just because she stood behind me."

"I'm not proud of that."

"But you did it."

"Yeah," Hawkins said. "I did it."

Maddox's bull reared up inside him. *He tried to hurt our mate! We will trample him!*

For an instant, Maddox was tempted to do just that. No

matter what reasons Hawkins had, he wasn't a good man. He'd done terrible things.

But so did I, once.

"You wanna make me a deal?" Maddox said. "I'm after your boss. I'm not even gonna ask you to help me get him. I just want you to stay out of my way. And no more messing with Verity or anybody else in town. They're under my protection now. Whole damn town's under my protection."

"You just pointed out that I'm not the one calling the shots," Hawkins said tightly. "So what happens when Ducker gives me orders to the contrary?"

"What happens is you figure out a way around it. Or you leave town. Man like you's bound to have some of those fat wads of cash salted away somewhere. You deny it?" Hawkins didn't speak. "Yeah, I thought so. If it comes down to it, you can take your wife and your payout, and start over somewhere else. That's a better ending that what'll happen to you if you mess with one more person in that town. Especially Verity Breslin."

Hawkins didn't answer.

Maddox shifted. It was starting to tire him out; every shift took a little energy. But it was clear that Hawkins needed a bit of encouragement. This time, with one large hoof planted on Hawkins' chest, Maddox tilted his head so the sharp tip of one of his long horns pressed against Hawkins' throat. He left it there just long enough to make his point, and then shifted back.

"Deal?" Maddox said. "As long as you stay out of my way —and let's be clear, messing with Verity or anybody else is sure as *hell* getting in my way—you and me can get along. If that doesn't happen, then I won't be this nice the next time."

"Deal," Hawkins said through tight lips.

Maddox leaned back and let him sit up. He held out his

hand, with the cuff dangling from his scraped-up wrist. After a long moment, Hawkins shook it.

"Now I'm gonna pick up your gun and hang onto it for safekeeping, and get my clothes, and we're both gonna drive back to town. Fair?"

"Fair," Hawkins said grimly. As Maddox got stiffly to his feet, he added, "Ducker's going to kill you, you know."

"Bigger men than him have tried and failed," Maddox said. "I'm not scared of him."

And he wasn't. Not anymore.

He reached a hand down to help Hawkins up. The sheriff stared at it for a long moment before taking it.

"What the hell *are* you, anyway?" he asked as Maddox hoisted him effortlessly to his feet, taking the opportunity to display a little shifter strength.

"Something you don't want coming after you," Maddox said simply, and went to get his clothes, or at least what was left of them.

VERITY

The neighbors and firefighters trickled gradually out of her yard, but Verity was much too wired to go back to bed. Thanks to an internet search, she now had the numbers of half a dozen lawyers—with no idea how she might be able to pay for their services, but she'd find some way. But there was nothing she could do until their offices began to open.

And all the while, Maddox was in the sheriff's clutches; she could only imagine the terrible things that could be happening to him right now.

Cleaning often made her feel better, and there was certainly a lot of cleaning to be done. It was better than sitting around worrying until morning. She'd started examining the fire damage on the porch with her hands, determining what would need to be replaced, when tires crunched at the curb.

Verity turned. She'd finally managed to stop obsessively checking the time, but she didn't think it was morning yet. "Hello?"

"Verity?" Maddox's voice said, and she let out a tiny cry and threw herself into his arms.

He hugged her back fiercely. He smelled like dirt and blood and the outdoors, but he was here, he was okay, he wasn't locked in a jail cell or lying in a shallow grave in the desert.

The vehicle that had dropped him off pulled away. "Who was that?" Verity asked.

"Sheriff Hawkins. We've got an understanding."

"*Hawkins*? What do you mean?"

"I mean he's going to leave us alone," Maddox said. "At least I'm reasonably confident he will. If he doesn't, I'll deal with him."

"But *how*? Did you—pay him off?"

Maddox laughed quietly, a rumble that she felt more than heard; she still had her arms locked tight around him. "No, we just discussed things, and he decided leaving me alone was less trouble than being my enemy. It's Ducker who's the real problem, not him."

Verity's hands had found the ragged mess of his shirt, the stickiness of blood at his wrists, and her blood began to boil. "Did the sheriff do this?"

"I mostly did it to myself, getting out of the handcuffs. It's not as bad as it probably feels to you," he added quickly, with the same odd undertone that he often got when he talked about any of his injuries. She knew a lot of men had trouble admitting physical weakness, but Maddox must have a world-class case of it to get so weird about it. "It's almost healed already," he added.

And there he went again. "If it just happened an hour or two ago, it can't possibly be."

"I told you, I'm a fast healer."

"You sure are." She shook her head in disbelief.

"Verity ..." Maddox began, and then he stopped, like he'd

changed his mind about what he wanted to say. "I think I'm going to need a new shirt. I kinda destroyed the one you gave me."

"Come on. There's plenty more where that came from. And we can get your wrists cleaned up."

They went around the side of the house with their arms still around each other. "I'd feel a lot better if you'd go away for awhile," Maddox said. "Go stay with Bailey, or better yet, you two get a hotel for awhile, somewhere far away from here."

"Not a chance," Verity said firmly. "If nothing they've done so far has run me off, *this* isn't going to change that."

"They could have killed you!"

"I'm not afraid," she told him. "Not with you here to protect me."

"Verity, listen—"

"No, you listen. I've been dealing with Ducker and Hawkins by myself for a long time. You've only been in town for a couple of days, and you've already made Hawkins back off. At this rate, you should have Ducker out of our hair in a week or two."

He gave a faint chuckle. "Pretty high opinion of me you got there."

"You've earned it."

She could feel him limping heavily, and she let him go up the stairs ahead of her. As she swiped a hand to touch his leg, she was startled to find his jeans in rags; he must be barely decent.

"Okay, I understand your shirt being torn up, but how did the sheriff do this to your jeans?" She could only think of a few ways his clothes could get torn up like that, all of them terrible. "Did he *drag* you?"

"We scuffled and both of us got pretty wrecked on the rocks."

But that evasive quality was back in his voice.

"Well, you're going to need new ones. I don't know if I have anything that'll fit you—oh, I know what I can do. I'll go next door and borrow something from a neighbor."

"Not right now," he said quietly, reaching back to capture her hand in his. "I just want you with me for awhile."

They showered together, Verity gently bathing his scrapes and other hurts, as he washed the smoke-smell off her. And then they fell into bed together, and he was right, there was definitely no need for pants until morning.

V erity had hoped to sleep in, but the phone calls and knocks on the door began at first light.

Before too long, she'd talked to the town reporter, another reporter from a county paper, her insurance company, and every neighbor who had somehow managed to sleep through the fire trucks and impromptu block party down the street. In the middle of it all, she found the time to run over to Ed and Betty's, and came away with an armload of men's clothing they'd been planning to take to the Goodwill. Ed wasn't as tall as Maddox, but he was a hefty guy, and she left Maddox sorting through the pile while she went downstairs to deal with yet another concerned neighbor.

Which was why she was out on the porch when Ducker showed up.

"Good morning, Ms. Breslin," his smooth, cultured voice declared, and Verity stopped in the act of reaching for her front doorknob. "I hear you had some trouble last night."

"Yes," she said coolly, turning around. "Yes, we did. Are you here alone, or do you have your pet sheriff along?"

"It's just me." His footsteps tip-tapped up the porch steps, no doubt the sound of expensive Italian leather shoes. Verity reminded herself that, as far as she knew, Ducker had never been violent himself. He preferred to pay other people to do his violence for him. Still, she wished Maddox would come downstairs.

As if he had somehow sensed her nervousness, she instantly heard his heavy tread on the back steps, and smiled to herself.

"As you can see, Mr. Ducker," she said, "I'm quite busy cleaning up the damage from last night. If you'd like to help out ..." She held out a broom in his direction and was unsurprised when no hand took it from her.

Maddox's arrival was announced with stomping footsteps and a growled-out, "What the hell are *you* doing here?"

"Oh good, Mr. Murphy." If anything, Ducker's voice became even smoother and plummier; Verity distrusted it immediately. "You're both here. That'll save some time."

"You want me to throw this guy off your property, Verity?" Maddox asked. His tone suggested he'd be more than happy to.

Verity was tempted, but she didn't want to give Ducker cause to sue Maddox or have him arrested (again). She crossed her arms. "Let's find out what he wants."

Maddox touched her arm lightly and then his arm slid around her. "You heard the lady. Talk."

"Not going to invite me in for a cup of tea?" Ducker asked lightly, and was met with stony silence from both of them. "Ah well. This is mainly information that I think Ms. Breslin would like to know, though you may find this conversation enlightening as well, Mr. Murphy." Papers rustled. "I had an interesting chat with Sheriff Hawkins this morning."

"Yeah, I'll bet," Maddox muttered.

"You seemed to make *quite* the impression on him. I wouldn't exactly say he's scared of you, but it was not a topic he wanted to discuss. However, I decided it was worth digging into your past a bit more, and I found a number of fascinating things."

Verity felt Maddox's arm give a convulsive jerk against her. His voice was steady, though, keeping its low, threatening register. "Everybody's got some stuff in their past."

"Oh, but few people have a past like *you*, Mr. Murphy. I assume you've come clean with your ladyfriend, haven't you?"

"Maddox?" Verity said. "What's he talking about?"

"Oh, you *haven't*." Ducker sounded so smugly satisfied that she yearned to reach out and slap him.

"What he's talking about is that I used to do the kind of work Hawkins does for him," Maddox said, the words tumbling out hastily. "Protection work, that kind of thing."

"Oh, *that*," Verity said. "I knew that. I guessed it, anyway." But she was apprehensive nonetheless. Ducker sounded awfully confident. She couldn't imagine anything he could possibly say changing her mind about Maddox, but—what dirt *had* he dug up, anyway?

Remember that he's a lying snake, she reminded herself. *He's not necessarily going to say anything that's true.*

"Oh, it's a lot more than that," Ducker was saying smoothly. Papers shuffled again. "I suppose you can't look at this, Ms. Breslin—*such* a shame—but your boyfriend has all kinds of interesting job skills. Shakedown rackets. Interrogations. Driver and bagman for mafia bosses. And he has the felony record to prove it."

Remember that you guessed most of this already. Remember that he's going to make sure that anything true sounds as bad as possible.

"Maddox, how much of this is true?" she asked.

Maddox's voice was heavy. "All of it."

He started to step away from her, but she grabbed his

arm. "Don't go anywhere," she said fiercely, and told Ducker, "I already know what kind of man Maddox is. Whoever he was in the past, he's the man who's running for sheriff of this town, and he's going to be a far, far better sheriff than Hawkins ever was. He'll protect this town from men like Hawkins, and men like you."

"Yes, well, if you change your mind—" There was a creak on the porch of Ducker moving toward them, and she felt Maddox surge forward, followed by the sounds of a slight scuffle. "If you *don't mind*," Ducker snapped indignantly, "I just want to give the lady something."

"She doesn't want anything from you."

"I'll answer for myself, thanks," Verity said. "What does he have?"

"It's one of those little keychain computer things."

"A flash drive? What's on it?" she asked, addressing the question to Ducker.

"The results of my investigations into your boyfriend." Ducker descended the porch steps with quick taps of his shoes. "I'm just going to leave it on your porch railing here. You can listen to it if you want, or not, at your discretion."

Verity stood with her hand lightly touching Maddox's back as he kept his bulk in front of her. Ducker's footsteps receded, and a car door slammed.

"He's gone?" she asked quietly as the car's tires crunched on the street.

"He's gone," Maddox confirmed.

Verity went to the edge of the porch and ran her fingers along the railing until they encountered a small, hard object. Then she dropped it under her foot and crunched it very hard, several times, with the heel of her shoe.

"Verity—" Maddox began.

"It's not that I don't care about it," she said, turning

127

toward him. "It's that I don't want to hear it from him. I want to hear it from you."

With that, she went to the door, aware of a whisper of air as Maddox moved out of the way. She brushed her fingertips across the charred wood around the frame. The door no longer closed properly, and she had to push hard to open it as it stuck in the warped frame. She was going to need some significant repairs to the front of the building, but that was something to deal with later.

"I'm going to make tea," she said over her shoulder. "And then we'll talk."

$$\sim$$

They took the tea out to the garden. By now the sun was high and the day was getting warm. Not too warm, though; summer's heat had finally broken, and she looked forward to the cooler days of winter.

"I'm not sure what you want to know," Maddox said.

"I want to hear what would have been on that flash drive, but without Ducker's spin. I trust you, Maddox, and I believe you haven't lied to me, but there's a lot you haven't told me, too." She stopped, waiting for his response, but his silence was tacit agreement. "I want the rest now. I'm not going to base a relationship on half-truths. Tell me about yourself."

After a long silence, Maddox said, "I started working for the mob as a kid. My ma was dead, my old man was in prison, and I had an 'in' with the outfits because my dad used to do some work for them. At first it was just simple stuff, fetching and carrying, being a lookout, and when I got a little older, driving people around. But you know what I—" He stopped and gave a little laugh. "No, actually, you *don't* know what I look like, do you? I'm a big guy."

Despite herself, Verity had to smile. She reached out and

squeezed the first part of him in reach, the thick mass of his forearm. "I do know that much about you, Maddox."

Maddox huffed a small laugh. "Yeah. I guess you do. So I started getting tapped for protection work pretty quickly. By that I mean not just bodyguarding but ... er ..."

"Protection rackets?"

"Yes," he said softly. "I'm forty-three years old, Verity, and I've spent nearly all of my life doing that kind of work. For a long time, my job was to make problems go away for my employers. Any kind of problems. And I did it however it needed to be done. Eventually things went the way these things do. I got arrested and sent to prison for armed robbery. Did ten years in the federal pen. That's where I got a lot of the ink."

"Ink?"

"Oh," he said, sounding surprised. "I have tattoos. I'm sorry, I forgot you can't see them."

He took her hand and put it on his chest. "There's a bull here." His hand moved slowly along with hers. "And a dragon here. And here—a rose."

She traced the hard curve of his pecs with her fingertips and adjusted her mental image to include the sweep and curl of ink. "How long ago was that?" she asked gently.

"The tattoos? Or—"

"Any of it."

"I got my first tat when I was just a kid. The prison thing, though—I got out about seven, seven and a half years ago."

He hesitated, perhaps expecting condemnation, perhaps just looking for a cue to continue. "What did you do then?" she asked.

"I went looking for work. Honest work this time. I was going to get out of the business. But ..." With her hand on his arm, she felt him shrug. "When you have a felony record and look like me, nobody's going to hire you, especially when all your job skills come down to basically scaring people for money. Eventually I lucked into a job with a guy named Darius Keegan."

"What's he like?"

"A lot like Ducker," Maddox said. "Well, he used to be. Then. He's changed a lot. But the things I did for him ... they're the same kind of things Hawkins does for Ducker. You wanted to know why Hawkins is leaving us alone now? It's because we had a chat, as one gangster's strongman to another. Ducker is blackmailing him, so he's even got an excuse. I never had that. I just did it for the money. Because it was my job."

Self-loathing curled around the words. Verity opened her mouth to say that it was all right—and then stopped herself, because it *wasn't* all right, no matter how much she wanted to make it all right for him.

"Nothing can undo the things you did," she said. "But I can tell how hard you're working to change. Running for sheriff isn't just about getting rid of Hawkins for you, is it? It's about wanting to be a better person. Someone who works to keep people safe, not someone who makes them *less* safe."

"Yeah. It's about that. Some of it. Some of it's about wanting to change for you, too—to be a man who's worthy of you." He said it like it was no big deal, oblivious to the way it made her heart swell and warm in her chest. "I *hate* the things I did. I'd go back and change it if I could, but it's like you said, nobody can do that. So yeah, I want to fix this town. I want to fix me. I want ..." He stopped, and then said in a different voice, a hard and decisive voice, "I want to stop lying to you, Verity. It's not right."

She tightened her grip on his arm. "You haven't ever lied to me. I know you've skirted around the edge of the truth, but nothing you just told me is anything I hadn't guessed for myself. Maybe I didn't know the extent of it, but nothing you've told me has come as a huge shock."

"No," Maddox said, sounding frustrated. "You're wrong. I *have* been lying to you, mostly just by not telling the truth, but sometimes directly to your face. I hate it. You're right, a relationship can't be built on half-truths and lies. And whatever was on that little computer thingie—most of it's probably about the mob thing, but there might be something else. I don't know if he told Ducker, but there's something Hawkins knows about me that you don't."

She was getting nervous now. If his deep dark secret wasn't that he used to work for the mob, what else *could* there be? "Whatever this is," she began cautiously, "are you sure you want to tell me?"

"Yes. 'Cause if Hawkins knows, then Ducker might know, and if Ducker knows, you'll find out sooner or later anyway. Hell, the whole town might know soon. I wouldn't put it past that assh—er—that jerk to put up a billboard telling everybody about it." He jumped up suddenly. Verity, startled, got to her feet as well. She could hear him pacing in front of her. "I just didn't think this through ... like always. Planning's never been something I'm good at. But I do know this, Verity." He stopped pacing and took her by the shoulders, firmly but gently. "I never want to lie to you again. From here on out, there's only gonna be truth between us. Okay?"

"Okay," she agreed, but she couldn't help feeling even more anxious now. The question beat like a drum inside her head: *What else could it possibly BE?*

"Everything I just told you is the absolute truth. But I left out a few things. The biggest thing I left out is what Darius Keegan really is. He's a dragon."

He paused like he expected her to know what that meant. "Is that some kind of mob term?" she asked cautiously. "I don't know the slang from your world, Maddox. You're going to just have to tell me in plain English."

"I'm trying," he said. "I don't mean dragon as slang for something else. I mean, he's a dragon. Big and scaly, has wings and claws, flies around and hoards gold and jewels."

What on Earth, she thought. She wasn't sure whether to be angry at him, or worried about him. They'd been having a very serious conversation about his past and then ... this. "Maddox, if this is a joke, I'm afraid I'm not getting it. It's been a *very* long night."

"It's not a joke. It's the honest truth. Darius and his entire family are dragons. My family used to work for them—well, for Darius, specifically. He's over two hundred years old. My family quit working for him and moved to Jersey a long time ago, but it was those family connections that helped me get work with him after I got out of prison."

Did he actually *believe* this, or was he using it as some kind of bizarre metaphor? "You know dragons aren't real, right?"

"That's what everyone thinks. They're as real as you and me. They're as real as ..." He stopped, and sucked in a sudden breath, dropping his hands from her shoulders. "As real as people who turn into animals."

"Oh," she said with a tiny laugh. "*That* real, are they?"

"That's right." There were little rustling sounds in front of her, and then the zip of a zipper, and she realized suddenly that he was taking his clothes off.

"Maddox! What are you doing?"

"It's a good thing you have a nice high fence around this garden. I don't have to go anywhere else to show you this. Or ... no, I forgot, you can't see it, so you're going to have to feel it."

He took her hand and guided it to his bare shoulder.

By now she was completely and utterly baffled. Was it possible he was having some kind of psychotic break? Could that just *happen* to a person? "I wish you'd stop babbling about dragons and just tell me what I'm supposed to be feeling!"

"This," Maddox said.

There was a sound, but she had no idea what it was. It was organic, that was for sure, but she'd never heard anything like it before: a sort of quiet crinkling, or ripping, or maybe gurgling, like soft things were moving past each other, pushing against each other.

His shoulder heaved under her hand. Heaved, and flexed, and—expanded? It was very sudden; the lurch of his shoulder pushed her back a step, and when she tightened her fingers to keep from being knocked over, there was a whole lot more shoulder to hold onto.

And it was furry.

Now utterly baffled, she explored with her fingers. If she didn't know any better, she'd think she had her hand on the shoulder of some sort of animal. It just went up and up. It was almost like touching a fur coat, except it was clearly alive, because she could feel it moving under her hand with the slight movements everyone makes as they keep themselves balanced. She could feel the ripple of muscles, the hardness of bone.

And she might have thought it was some sort of stupid sleight-of-hand trick—that he'd slipped something else under her hand and fled—except that didn't seem like him, and also, she could hear him breathing.

Or ... she could hear *something* breathing.

It was big and deep, a slow gusty bellows, in and out. And now that she thought about it, she could feel each gusty breath tickle her hair from ... above?

Very hesitantly, very nervously, she put up the hand that

was not currently resting on the warm fur of ... *whatever* was in front of her.

She touched warm moistness and jerked her fingers back, at the same time as she heard a loud, very animal-like snort from above her and felt the warm furriness flinch and ripple.

"What," she said out loud, very faintly.

She reached up again, more slowly this time. She had petted cows and sheep—she lived in farm country, after all—so she now recognized the warm, damp feeling of some sort of large animal breathing on her. She touched its soft, moist nose.

"M—Maddox?"

The ... whatever-it-was gave a snort. Somehow it *sounded* like Maddox.

Disbelieving, she explored his face with her fingers. It felt like some kind of ... cow? There was a broad furry forehead, the fringe of eyelashes, a shaggy topknot almost like a horse's mane. She touched the smooth curve of what felt like enormous horns, each as big around as her fist at the base.

And then suddenly there was that same weird popping/crackling noise and she had her hand on a man's face.

Verity jumped back, stumbling into her chair. The lawn furniture knocked into each other, and someone's teacup went over and hit the stone edging of a flowerbed with a crunch and tinkle of porcelain.

"Oh, no. I'm so sorry." Maddox caught her gently, and then his voice moved as he knelt to pick it up. "Jeez. I didn't mean to."

"Maddox ..." She touched his bare shoulder. It was nothing but normal skin, the smooth well-muscled feeling of a male back. It was hard to believe she hadn't been ... what? Fantasizing, dreaming?

No. She'd felt what she'd felt, fur and muscle and bone and horn, and the warm breath of some kind of large animal.

"What *was* that?" she asked. Her voice came out small and plaintive. In a world where she couldn't rely on her eyes, relied instead on the touch of her fingers, she depended upon the certainty that the world around her would remain well-organized and reliable. Items would be where she left them. The floor would be there under her feet. Men did not just turn into large shaggy animals in front of her ... "What *are* you?"

"I'm a bull. Uh ... a really big, shaggy bull. Like a Highland kind of bull."

"I ... I don't understand," Verity said faintly.

Maddox caught her arm and guided her to a chair. "You okay? This cup is smashed up pretty bad, but I got all the glass—it's here on the table—"

"I don't care about the cup." She started to jerk her arm out of his grasp, but stopped, because she needed to know where he was—and what he was turning into. "Tell me about the cow."

"Bull," Maddox corrected. "A cow is female—"

"I know a cow is female! Maddox!" She grabbed his arm with her other hand, clinging to his solidity and trying not to remember the feeling of his body rearranging itself under her hands. "People can't just—turn into things! What *else* can you turn into?"

"Nothing else. Just my bull." He paused; it was almost like he was listening to something she couldn't hear. "Listen, I know it's hard to believe. We're called shifters. Most humans don't know about us."

"And you used to work for a dragon."

"Yeah," Maddox said.

Verity gave a strangled laugh. She pulled out of his grip and buried her face in her hands.

Maddox's touch hovered lightly against her upper arms, just the barest brushes of his fingertips. "Uh ... are you okay?"

"No!" she squawked out. She lowered her hands when she was entirely sure she wasn't going to burst into tears or hysterical laughter. "You turned into a ... a *cow*!"

"Bull," Maddox corrected patiently. "Yeah, you wanted to know how my clothes got all torn up. That's how."

"And why Hawkins was willing to leave us alone on your say-so."

"Well, it's not just that—we did have a talk—"

"*Maddox*."

"Yeah," he said, sounding slightly embarrassed. "I turned into a bull and kinda trampled him a little. Just a little."

Verity squawked out another strangled laugh and buried her face in her hands again.

"Verity ..."

She took a long, slow breath through her fingers, lowered her hands, and squared her shoulders. "Maddox, it has been a very long, very awful night. I'd like to be alone for a little while."

His hands left her shoulders, and she sensed a change in the warmth of the sunlight on her face: he'd stood up, blocking the sun. "Do you want me to ... go? I mean, to leave. Permanently."

No, cried her heart, but mostly she was just horribly, horribly confused. It felt like the ground had tilted under her feet, like she'd reached for her phone and found out it had turned into a spatula or a bar of soap. "I don't know," she said. "Just ... please leave me alone for now."

There was an intake of breath like he'd started to say something, and then he said quietly, "Yes, ma'am."

His feet crunched on the gravel path as he walked away from her.

MADDOX

Maddox got dressed on the back patio. He had the presence of mind to retrieve his cane from where he'd left it, what seemed like forever ago now, mainly because his hip ached with a grinding pain that threatened collapse if he tried to go very far on it. And right now, he needed to walk.

He needed to leave.

He looked back at Verity sitting in the sun-drenched garden, with her head in her hands. *He'd* done that.

We need to go back! his bull protested. *Our mate is distressed; we must comfort her!*

Shut up, Maddox thought viciously at it. None of this was his bull's fault, but right now, it felt like it.

He walked through the shop with its shelves in disarray, and out the front door, askew on its hinges; across the blackened boards of the porch, down to the front walk where her careful plantings were trampled, and blackened streams of dried-up hose water ran from the porch across the sidewalk to the gutters.

Her beautiful shop was a wreck—he'd done that. He

broke everything he touched. It was his one big job skill; why did he think meeting his mate would make things any different?

He limped away from Verity's house into the sunlit morning. Dimly, he was aware that it was a beautiful day, the sky nearly cloudless but the breeze cool enough to make it pleasant and comfortable. But he registered this with only a dim corner of his mind.

Several people waved to him and called out greetings from yards and porches. He grunted distracted acknowledgement and limped on, out of the town proper, onto the road to the highway. Past the place where he'd nearly died in the ditch. Onward, to the highway and its gravel shoulder where the truck had let him off mere days ago.

It seemed like a lifetime ago.

He wasn't sure where he was going. He just needed to get away.

On the shoulder of the highway, he stopped and looked back, across rolling ranch country and stands of trees toward the cluster of buildings that marked the town.

So you're just going to run away, leave them to deal with Ducker all on their own. Leave her *to deal with it.*

He wasn't sure if that was the voice of his bull or his conscience.

I'm not running. I'm putting some distance between me and them—between me and Verity—for their own good.

He had to take on Ducker himself. It was the only way. And to do that, he needed to make sure that Ducker didn't have anyone to use against him as leverage ... because Ducker *absolutely* would.

He started walking again, limping slowly, his hip grinding.

Could he pull the same thing on Ducker that he had on Hawkins? Just turn into a bull and threaten him? No ... he rejected the idea immediately. He'd read Hawkins as a bully and a thug, who would back down as soon as someone managed to prove they were bigger and meaner than he was, but people like Ducker were different. They were used to throwing their weight around in a whole different way. Maddox thought about what Darius Keegan would do if someone crossed him like that. He wouldn't back down, that was for sure. He'd probably record Maddox's transformation somehow and try to blackmail him. Or he might kidnap Verity and try to hurt her.

No, he couldn't use violence to get Ducker off his back. He'd only play into Ducker's hands that way.

So what else can I do?

He heard an engine coming up behind him, and looked over his shoulder nervously. It wasn't the sheriff this time, just a long-haul big-rig cruising down the highway. Although he hadn't stuck his thumb out, the truck's air brakes hissed, and it pulled over on the shoulder just ahead of him. The trucker leaned out the rolled-down window. "Hey, buddy. Need a lift?"

He could say yes. For a moment it was tempting.

He could go wherever the big-rig was going, to Flagstaff or Phoenix or even farther away. He'd have a chance to regroup and consider his options and make plans—far away from Verity, where his presence couldn't put her in even more danger.

And all Verity would know was that he'd run away.

No, he thought.

No, he was done running. He had been running for months, ever since he'd been injured and had quit working for Darius. He had run and run, always telling himself he was going toward something, never quite able to admit he was running away instead.

He waved the trucker onward. The truck pulled back out

onto the highway, and Maddox turned away from the road and limped down into the ditch. He ducked under strands of fencing. There was a cluster of boulders shaded by some trees, and he sat on a big rock and massaged his hip while a cluster of distant cattle watched him curiously.

As he was sitting there, his phone vibrated.

His first thought was: *Verity!* He pulled it out and looked. As if his past had decided to catch up with him in the most blatant way possible, there was a text message from Loretta, Darius's mate.

He had gotten a couple of texts from Darius over the months since he'd left, most notably an invitation to his and Loretta's wedding, which Maddox had regretfully declined and said he was busy. (He'd been in Montana at the time, and not at all busy, but he couldn't imagine facing them after vanishing for months.) In general, Darius seemed happy enough to let Maddox go his separate way.

Loretta, on the other hand ...

She'd never stopped texting, never stopped emailing. Even though Maddox only sent back an occasional, short reply, Loretta soldiered on with the kind of never-say-die persistence that allowed her to be happily married to the most stubborn man Maddox had ever met. He still got a new text or email from her almost every week, a new photo of the half-finished house she and Darius were building to replace their destroyed one, a picture of their cat, a photo of a flower or a sunset.

She never asked him where he was. She just said things like *I hope you're doing well,* or *We think about you a lot.*

This was another text with a picture attached, black-and-white and blurry. He couldn't even tell what it was, turning the phone this way and that, but it stayed indistinct. He didn't realize what it was until he read her message:

6 mos checkup went great! We know the baby's sex now, but we aren't telling. ;) Say hi to your godbaby.

That's right. Loretta was pregnant. This was a sonogram.

He stared at it for a long while. It still didn't look much like a baby to him. And he thought about Loretta, whose life he'd helped save, and who had never forgotten it.

Say hi to your godbaby.

Then he took a slow breath and pressed the number to call her back.

It rang a couple of times on the other end, and then Loretta's voice, light and warm with a hint of a drawl, said delightedly, "Maddox! Hi! Hold on, let me sit down."

"I hope this isn't a bad time to call. You just texted me, so I figured—"

"No—no! Not at all." There was a clatter and thump in the background. "I was just chopping peppers. I'm trying to make ratatouille, because we watched the movie yesterday at the preschool—you know, the one with the actual rats—and the kids wanted to know what it tastes like, so I said I'd make some and bring it in. Except I've never made it, or actually eaten it, and now I wish I'd just done what Darius said and ordered some from a restaurant and brought that instead—" She broke off with an embarrassed laugh. "Maddox, I'm sorry. We haven't heard from you in ages, and here I am, rambling like I do. How are you?"

Was *that* ever a question that didn't have a simple answer. The answer just dropped out. "I met my mate."

Loretta's shriek made him hold the phone away from his ear.

"That's fantastic!" she was saying as he put it back. "I can't wait to tell Darius. Wow. What's her name? What's she like? Is she a shifter?"

"She's human, and her name is Verity, and ... she's perfect."

Loretta's delighted laugh burbled up. "Okay, that sounds

like a shifter in love, all right. So tell me more about her, other than how perfect she is. Where are you?"

"I'm in Arizona. A town called Silvermine. Verity runs a tea shop here." Remembering belatedly that he hadn't actually said anything about the sonogram yet, he added, "Thanks for the text. That's, uh, it looks like a great baby. Um. Very pretty?"

Loretta laughed again. "Maddox, it's a gray blur. You'll just have to take my word there's a baby in there somewhere. I don't even know how the technician who reads the things can find arms and legs, let alone tell that it's a—" She broke off quickly. "But we're not telling anyone that, so you'll just have to be surprised in three months along with everyone else."

"You know, Maddox is a good name." It was hard not to be drawn along with her playful teasing. "For a boy or a girl."

"Oh no, if you think I'm naming my daughter Maddox, you have another think coming, mister. You'll have to do that with your own daughter. If you have one. Which you might! Does Verity want kids? Or is that getting ahead of your-selves? I know shifters move fast. Once you find the one, it's the *one*."

"We've kinda had other things going on than talking about kids," Maddox said uncomfortably. "She's got one, anyway. I mean, not her actual daughter, but her sister's daughter that she's raising. Her name is Bailey and she's a teenager."

"Wow, insta-teen! That's parenting on hard mode, buddy."

"I dunno, I've heard they're a lot of work when they're babies too."

"You'll have to find out. You're invited to babysit, you know. You have to come meet h—the baby," she caught herself quickly.

"You're not that great at keeping secrets, Miss Loretta," Maddox said, amusement chasing away some of his gloom.

"I *know*. I asked Darius if he wanted to maybe just have the nurse tell him and not me, because there's no *way* I can keep from telling anybody for three months, and if I tell any of my cousins it's going to be all over the trailer park before you know it, and telling the kids at the preschool, phew, forget it. But no, he said we're in this together, and he didn't want to know if I didn't know." Her voice melted into a besotted tone that Maddox had a feeling was what he probably sounded like when he talked about Verity.

"How is the boss—er, Darius?" It was still a little difficult, sometimes, to remember that he didn't work for the man anymore.

"He's good. We're good. Still working on the new—well, he adamantly refuses to call it a lair, but it's coming along." There were clinking sounds in the background; it sounded like she'd gone back to working on her ratatouille. "But Maddox, our lives are pretty boring right now compared to yours! It's just work and construction on the new mansion and me dealing with swollen ankles and fatigue—at least the morning sickness is over, thank God for that. You found your mate! You're in Arizona! You're a kinda-sorta surrogate dad for her teenage daughter! Isn't that amazing? Can you text me a picture?"

"Not really. Not right now. I kinda don't know if she's going to want to see me again."

There was a silence at the other end of the line, though cooking-related clinking let him know she hadn't hung up. Then Loretta said, in a voice that was warm and very gentle, "Do you want to talk about it?"

He hadn't had the slightest intention of getting Darius and Loretta involved in his problems. This wasn't their fight. They had been through enough of their own problems, and now they had a baby on the way and a good life they'd built for themselves in the (literal) ashes of Darius's old life.

They didn't need to be dragged into something that wasn't their fight.

But he was just so ... *tired*, and so desperately, achingly alone. And Loretta had always been easy to talk to.

"I'm still listening," she prompted in that same soft, gentle voice, and slowly, haltingly, he began to talk, pouring out the story of Verity and the sheriff, Ducker and the town of Silvermine.

Loretta made occasional sympathetic noises, offering no judgment or advice. Eventually he wound down with, "And now I'm sitting in a field outside town and I think she's scared of me and I guess I'm going to have to go fight Ducker soon."

"Oh, Maddox." Her voice was so filled with warmth that he didn't even feel embarrassed about having bared his soul to her. If she'd been here, she would probably have tried to hug him, and he thought he would probably have let her. The sound of her voice was almost like a hug. "*Maddox*. You're part of our family, and you always will be, no matter how far away you go. You don't have to deal with this all alone."

His throat tightened, and he swallowed, staring across the field until his eyes stopped burning. He didn't even remember the last time he'd cried. When his father died, maybe, a very long time ago. "I didn't want to get you guys mixed up in this."

"We're in it because you're in it. That's how family works."

His eyes stung again. "Look, even if you wanted to help, I don't know how much you can do. Maybe back in the old days, when Darius was richer than sin. But he's not like that anymore. I don't think he can take on Ducker in a business kind of way, and I don't want him to feel like he has to ..."

He stopped, not sure how much Loretta knew of the

darker side of her mate's past. She gave a soft, rueful laugh, and he thought, *Of course she knows.* They were mates. No part of their souls was ugly to the other.

But knowing it was one thing; bringing it down on their heads was another. Darius's past of violence and bloodshed had nearly gotten both him and his mate killed. And dragging Darius back into that, when he had a new life and a mate and a child on the way, was the last thing Maddox wanted to do.

"Yeah," Loretta said, as if he'd spoken aloud. "I don't think we want to tell Darius, not quite yet. He's going to need to know, for sure, but right now he'd want to—"

"Yeah."

"Dragons and small towns and ... it'd be a mess."

"Yeah."

"So it's you and me, then," Loretta said briskly, and now it was Maddox's turn to bark out a sharp laugh.

"What do you think Darius is going to do if he finds out I got his pregnant mate mixed up in all of this? You stay right where you are, Miss Loretta, and don't you dare lift a finger to do anything that might get Ducker after you."

"My gosh, you're assertive now that you don't work for us anymore. I like it," she said with a smile in her voice. "Don't worry, I'm not planning on dropping everything and rushing down there. In fact, there's not much I can do directly at all. But—Maddox—don't take this the wrong way, but have you thought at all that maybe we aren't the ones who should be handling this in the first place?"

"Huh?" Maddox said intelligently.

"From everything you've told me, Ducker and the sheriff are getting up to a lot that's illegal in that town. Sure, he's not breaking any laws just buying property on Main Street. But there certainly are laws against using the kinds of strong-arm tactics you're telling me about. Arson, for one, and attempted murder. They tried to have you killed, Maddox! There are definitely laws against *that*!"

"You're saying call the cops?" It was a completely alien thought to him. He'd spent his entire life trying to avoid law enforcement as much as possible. "But the sheriff *is* the cops."

"He's not the only one in the state," Loretta pointed out. "Or the country. This is what the FBI is for. And district attorneys, and that sort of thing. A corrupt sheriff isn't allowed to run a town as his own private little fiefdom. That's not how this country is supposed to work."

"Huh," Maddox said. He genuinely hadn't even thought of it. "But why didn't Verity do that?"

"Maybe she was scared. Maybe she didn't think it would work. Maybe she didn't even think of it. Why don't you ask her?"

The thought sent a wave of simultaneous delight and despair through him. "She said she needed time."

"That doesn't mean *go away forever*, Maddox. You turned into a bull in front of her. She's going to need some time to process that. Ask me how well I dealt with Darius turning into a dragon in front of me for the first time. Or I should say, snatching me out of a burning building without my clothes. At least you didn't do anything like that to Verity."

Although Maddox had been around for most of Darius's courtship of Loretta, this was the first time it really hit him how disturbing and frightening it must have been for her to have her entire worldview turned upside down. Admittedly a bull, even a large one, wasn't quite as startling as a dragon. But Loretta and Darius had gotten through that, and now she was carrying a half-dragon baby.

His heart began, tentatively, to lift. Maybe he and Verity could get through this as well.

"Still there, hon?" Loretta asked, and he realized that, from her end of the line, he'd gone totally quiet.

"Yeah, sorry. Just thinking about some things."

"I hope so." But she didn't say it in a mean way; her voice was warm and affectionate. "If she's your mate, Maddox, then the two of you will find a way. Mates always do."

"So you think she'll listen if I go back and talk to her?"

"I think if you don't, you'll never know and you'll both regret it for the rest of your lives. You have to have faith in her, Maddox. Faith that she is the person you think she is."

"I do," Maddox said fervently.

"So prove it. Be brave. It's a different kind of bravery than fighting, but it doesn't take any less strength." She laughed softly. "More, even, for people like you and Darius. But I know you're up to the challenge. Because I have faith in you, too."

Maddox took a slow breath. His chest felt too full to contain all the feelings there. "So how about I go back and talk to Verity, and suggest maybe we go to—the FBI, I guess? What kind of feds do you talk to about this kind of thing? It's all foreign to me."

"The FBI sounds like a good place to start. They're breaking the law, Maddox. And you can do something about it, the right way."

"The right way," he murmured. It felt very strange, thinking about taking a problem to the authorities instead of handling it the way he'd always handled things, on his own.

But maybe it was time to try living a different way. He didn't want to end up like Hawkins, taking orders from an evil man and telling himself he had no choice.

"You sound a lot better," Loretta said. "Sometimes talking it out helps, does it?"

"I guess it does. I never really had anyone to talk to about stuff before."

"Well," she said warmly, "now you do. It's like I told you earlier. You're family, and family helps each other out. Now get back there and have a proper conversation with your mate."

"Yes, ma'am," he said, smiling although she couldn't see him.

"And you tell me how it turns out, you hear?"

"Yes, ma'am."

He disconnected the call and stood in the sunlit field, filled with a sense of peace and ease that he hadn't had in a long time. Loretta was right, it *did* help to talk to someone, and she was also right that this was only a small bump on the road to happiness with Verity. They could get through it.

If I don't mess this up, that is.

He turned and began to limp back toward town.

VERITY

After Maddox's footsteps faded and the back door of the shop closed with a very final thunk, Verity slowly and mechanically began to clean up the broken cup and the rest of their tea things.

She was still trying to process everything she'd learned about Maddox this morning. She had known there was something different about him, something unlike anyone she'd ever met. She just hadn't realized how deep it ran.

She had no interest in opening the tea shop today. She left the door locked and the sign flipped to CLOSED. Instead she took her cane and went for a walk.

The sun was warm on her shoulders and face. She'd been walking around this town all her life, and today she simply wandered, trusting in her general knowledge of local geography to keep her from getting too lost. She needed the activity to keep pace with her buzzing thoughts, bouncing around from Maddox to the problem of Ducker and back to Maddox again.

She didn't think Maddox had gone for good. At least she hoped he hadn't. Her hand kept creeping toward her phone and then jerking away; finally she turned her phone off to remove the temptation to call him. She wasn't going to beg him to come back, or even ask. He had to come back on his own, or else he wasn't the man she thought he was.

Prove to me that you're a better man than your past makes you, Maddox. Come back to me so we can deal with this together.

In the meantime, she didn't plan to just sit around waiting for him to show up. She wondered if it was possible there was a way around Ducker that they hadn't found yet. Could something in the city's bylaws or property records provide a possible new avenue of attack? She hadn't even thought of looking there for a loophole that would enable them to escape Ducker's attempted land grab.

"Excuse me," she said to a set of brisk footsteps tapping her way. "Could you direct me to the city records office, please?"

One brief conversation later, she'd walked a block in the indicated direction and pushed open a door with a little bell that tinkled. She had gone in here occasionally in the course of running her own business, usually to file paperwork associated with her business.

"I need to do a records search. Can you do text to speech on these computers?" she asked.

The secretary showed her how to set it up and then left her alone. It wasn't nearly as nice a setup as the one she had at home; the computer droned at her in a mechanical voice, and she especially missed her Braille display, which would have allowed her to skim documents. Here she was forced to listen to the computer droning on and on, unable to skip ahead because she was afraid of missing something important. She didn't even know what she was looking for, just that there had to be *something*.

And, to her surprise, she found it.

She found it in a seemingly endless series of clauses and

subclauses in the town charter. As the computer droned about water rights and acreage and boundaries, she tried to force her mind not to wander. And then suddenly her thoughts sharpened to a laser focus. Had she really just heard what she thought she heard? She ran it back and listened again.

Then she called the secretary and asked if she could get these pages printed. A few minutes later, she was out on the sidewalk, waiting for a taxi.

$\sim$

D ucker's office was located in a big office building in the county seat. She'd been there once before when he had invited her to talk about selling her shop, back when she'd still believed that if she refused to sell, he would politely take no for an answer and look elsewhere.

On the taxi ride, she collected her thoughts. The paper rustled in her hand. It might be a bit of a long shot, but it was a better chance than anything she'd found so far.

The taxi let her out on the sidewalk in front of Ducker's office tower. She patted down her hair, tucking in her braids, and wished she'd taken the time to go home and change into something more professional-looking. She was wearing the light blouse and long skirt she'd put on this morning, when she planned to do nothing more than stick around the shop all day. Oh well; the important thing was the information she carried with her, and she'd learned in her life that confidence went a long way toward making up for other shortcomings. Reminding herself that right was on her side—legally and morally—she strode into the office.

Ducker's administrative assistant was a lot less helpful than the record-office secretary. "I'm sorry, ma'am. I can't let you in without an appointment."

"Then make an appointment for me."

There was a tapping of keys. "How does next week sound?"

"Today," Verity said.

"I'm sorry. I'm afraid that's not possible."

The carpets were so soft and thick in Ducker's outer office that Verity didn't even hear the approach of footsteps until Ducker's smooth, cultured voice said, "It's all right, Cindy. I'll make a few moments for Ms. Breslin."

Verity tried not to jump. "Thank you," she said, holding her head high.

"Right this way. Have a seat. Would you like coffee?"

"Tea, if you have it," she said, and took the offered seat, then used the opportunity to try to guess at the size and shape of the space around her, based on Ducker's whisper-soft steps—even now that she was listening, she had to strain to hear them—and the clinking of the coffee things. She listened carefully for other people around her, but she didn't think there were any, unless they were being extremely quiet. They appeared to be alone in a very large office. With the door to the outer office shut, she couldn't even hear his assistant going about the usual secretarial tasks. She tried not to feel trapped.

"Coffee only, I'm afraid. Cream? Sugar?"

"Both," she said, and accepted the cup he pressed lightly into her hand, inhaling the too-bitter steam.

The faint whisper of Ducker's steps circled around to the other side of his desk. Leather creaked as he sat down. "Now, Ms. Breslin, what's your business here? Dare I to guess that you've come to revisit my earlier purchase offer?"

"No, actually." She felt for the corner of his desk and set the coffee cup on it. "I'm here to tell you that I'm not selling to you, now or ever, and this is why I don't have to." She held out her folded copy of the town charter.

Ducker actually laughed. "Now, Ms. Breslin, I'm not sure what you think you've got there—"

"I know what I've got here." She shook the piece of paper at him. "This is a copy of the original town charter and bylaws, which are still in effect. When this town was founded, the city fathers were worried about having it become a company town, like a lot of other mining towns in the West. So they wrote some bylaws into the original paperwork to prevent it. No single owner, private or corporate, can own more than ten percent of the property or businesses within the town limits. I think you're already well over that limit, aren't you?"

There was a silence. Then she felt the piece of paper snatched out of her hand. "That's ridiculous," Ducker said, and the paper rustled as he unfolded it.

"Maybe, but it's also legally binding. I checked at the city records office. It's just not enforced much. Most people don't know about it. But if someone wanted to take you to court—especially if, say, a group of business owners got together and took you to court for violating the city charter—they would have a very good case. You'd have to actually get the bylaws changed, and that's a process that would take years and is entirely in the hands of the town council, most of whom don't like you very much."

The paper rattled against the edge of Ducker's desk. "This is completely absurd. An antiquated pipe dream written by a bunch of hillbillies a hundred years ago. You cannot possibly expect this to stand up in court."

"Really? That's not what the records office told me." She leaned forward, reveling in the feeling of power and strength. "The reason why I came here rather than going straight to a lawyer is because I wanted to give you a chance to quietly, off the books, return some of the property that you've taken from this town's honest businesspeople. If you don't, we will take you to court, and we will win. On top of that, your name will be dragged through the papers. You'll be known far and wide as the guy who tried to destroy a small-town Main Street and instead got taken to the cleaners by a bunch of, as you put it, *hillbillies*."

There was a tearing sound.

"Oh, very mature," Verity said. "You know that's a copy, right? The real charter is on file not just in the city records office but also with the county and in their computerized system. You can't destroy it."

"I don't need to do that," Ducker said. The paper crumpled and she heard it fall into a wastebasket. "I just need to make sure *you* don't get a chance to talk to anyone about it."

An icy chill snaked down her spine. "It's a matter of public record."

"Yes, but who knew about it before you found it? And who have you told?"

All of a sudden the weakness in her plan was suddenly, blindingly obvious. "My lawyer," Verity said quickly.

"Really? I don't think you have. I think you rushed straight over here, and now you're realizing that no one knows where you are, and no one knows about your unique discovery. Ms. Breslin, you have neatly trapped yourself."

Verity's palms began to sweat. She told herself to be calm. "What are you going to do, try to kidnap me? I'll scream."

"Really? Who will hear you? I own the entire floor, and everything is very well soundproofed. I am *very* fond of my privacy. But," he added, as Verity drew in her breath to make good on her screaming threat and also groped her way across the desk for something to use as a weapon, "there's absolutely no need for that kind of fuss and bother. We're both adults and we can come to a reasonable arrangement, I'm sure."

"What sort of arrangement?" Verity asked. Her fingers closed over a stapler. It felt large and heavy in her palm.

There was the sound of a drawer being opened and closed, followed by soft rustling on his desktop. "You won't be able to read this, of course," Ducker said in smoothly condescending tones, "but the papers I just put in front of you are a transfer of ownership of your shop to me. It has everything except your signature." There was a small plasticky click. "I just put a pen beside it."

"And what do I get if I sign?"

"Fair compensation, as agreed upon."

She didn't for a moment believe him. He could have her sign anything. Keeping a hand curled around the stapler, she said grimly, "So you won't mind if I take these papers to my lawyer and have him review them?"

Ducker sighed. "My dear, you know you haven't got a choice about signing these, don't you? You must realize you are not negotiating from a position of strength. From your reaction earlier, I can guess that no one knows you're here, and I've heard your protector left town."

"Then you heard wrong," Verity said flatly.

"Really? I have it from several reliable witnesses that he was seen walking out to the highway to hitch a ride this morning."

Had he really? She refused to believe it. "He's ... on an errand. For me."

"Is that right?" He sounded amused and skeptical.

"Yes," Verity said, putting as much confidence in her voice as she could. "Do you really think I'd come here without telling Maddox? He knows *exactly* where I am, and if I don't come back safely, he'll be very upset."

"Even if this is true, what do you think he's going to do? He's only one man." Leather creaked as Ducker rose from his chair again. "You two can't fight me. Let me show you why. Come with me."

Verity flinched away as he gripped her arm. It was very different from Maddox's light, guiding touches; this was a controlling grasp that she couldn't pull away from, almost hard enough to hurt. She kept her hand firmly wrapped around the stapler, and Ducker either didn't notice or didn't care enough to make a big deal about it. He assisted her out of the chair (dragged, rather) and guided her across the room.

"If you're taking me to a window, you should realize the view won't do anything for me," Verity said with bravado she didn't feel. He wouldn't push her out a window, would he? Surely not.

Ducker chuckled. "It's not a window." His hand guided hers. "It's this. Feel it."

Nervous but curious, Verity ran her fingertips across something odd, a series of blocky shapes. *Legos?* she thought, baffled. She found a small street sign with her fingers, and realized it was some kind of diorama set up in the corner of his office.

"What is this?"

"This," Ducker said proudly, "is the new Silvermine Industrial Park. Once I get all your land, I'll tear down that row of unsightly shacks, and put up something bright and modern. I already have investors lined up."

"Those 'unsightly shacks' are our historic downtown."

"No one cares. Main Street is dead these days, Ms. Breslin; don't you read the papers? Oh, wait, I forgot. You can't."

"I read the paper on my computer every morning," Verity said between her teeth.

"In any case, now you can see why your delaying tactics will come to nothing in the long run." He steered her back to the desk. Her hip bumped the chair, but she defiantly remained standing. "I already have most of the necessary permits and most of the land I need, minus a few holdouts like you. You can wave all the bits of paper at me that you want, but I have enough lawyers to make those problems go away. All I need is your land."

"Which I'll never sell to you."

"Oh, you will. You definitely will, and—" He broke off, and Verity tensed at the sound of the door opening. "*Finally.* What took you so long?"

"Sorry, boss," Hawkins' voice said, and Verity's stomach sank down to her toes.

"It's lucky for you that she didn't come here with a weapon, if you're going to take forever to provide the security I'm paying you for," Ducker said in clipped tones. "Now then, Ms. Breslin, it's time for you to sign these papers."

"No," Verity said.

A big hand closed around hers, pressing a pen into it. Verity wasn't sure if it was Ducker or Hawkins, but she didn't really care.

She lashed out with the stapler, swinging it at the approximate region where Ducker's voice had come from. There was a thunk, a jolt she felt up her arm, and a yell of shock and anger.

Verity grabbed for her cane, leaning beside her chair where she'd left it. It was a light, collapsible cane, designed to be easy to carry rather than having any kind of weapon potential, but she swung it anyway. There was a glassy crash as she knocked something off a desk or table, and then a crack as it hit something else, followed by a violent wrench that yanked it out of her hands.

"You little *bitch*!" Ducker's voice was muffled, the genteel facade completely gone. "My face! You and that animal Maddox deserve each other. Dammit, Hawkins, restrain her!"

Verity dived for the door, but she was brought up short

by a pair of big arms closing around her. She kicked and struggled as Hawkins pinned her arms to her sides.

"Calm down," Hawkins' voice said in her ear. His grip was surprisingly gentle, like he was trying not to hurt her.

"Yes, I suggest you do that," Ducker said behind her, approaching with a tread heavy enough that she could hear it clearly even on the soft carpet. "You don't want us to hurt your pretty little niece, do you?"

"Bailey?" The fight went out of her as horror filled her. They had Bailey?

Newly tractable, she put up no resistance as they hustled her out of the office, not the way she'd come but down another hallway that smelled different, and into an elevator. Her phone was taken from her before she could think of calling for help.

"You don't really have Bailey, do you?" she asked as the elevator sank, and with it, her hopes. "You were lying to get me to come with you."

"It worked, didn't it." Ducker's voice still sounded thick. She hoped she'd broken his nose.

The elevator doors slid open and Verity began to scream. "Help! Help me! I'm being kidnapped!"

"Nice try," Ducker said. His voice grew more distant. "This is a private parking garage, below the street. There's no one down here but us. Bring her to the car whenever she's done having her temper tantrum, Ted."

Hawkins' hands closed on her arms again. Verity made an effort to jerk away. Hawkins leaned in close, and she shuddered, trying to pull away. But when his breath ghosted across her neck, what he whispered was, "Don't fight me. I'm trying to help you. I'll tell your boyfriend where we took you."

Verity was afraid her bafflement was written all over her face, but if so, it must have been mistaken for fear. She allowed herself to be pushed into the backseat of Ducker's enormous truck. The door slammed, and then Ducker himself got in next to her, smelling like cigars and expensive cologne. The truck's engine started with a roar.

"You know why your dull little town is called Silvermine, don't you?" Ducker asked.

"Of course I do," Verity said. "There used to be mines around here."

"Correct. Technically, there still are."

She knew that too, but didn't bother pointing it out. Most of the old-time mines had been boarded up; some were parks or tourist attractions. Bailey liked to go hiking around the nearest ones. Verity had never been, preferring to stay close to town where there weren't rattlesnakes and unexpected holes in the ground.

The truck moved. Verity wondered if Hawkins had been telling the truth, or if he had merely said whatever he needed to say to get her to calm down and cooperate.

"We're going to one of those old mines right now." Ducker sounded very smug. "You don't mind the dark, Ms. Breslin? Where we're taking you, it's very dark. And no one is every going to find you."

MADDOX

In the short time Maddox had been gone, Verity seemed to have vanished into thin air.

He tried the shop first, but it was closed and locked. Her phone just went to voice mail. He hesitated to leave a message. Maybe later, if he couldn't locate her first, but he felt that he owed her a conversation in person.

If only he could find her to have that conversation.

He sank down wearily on the porch steps, resting his aching leg.

"What's wrong, son?" asked one of Verity's elderly neighbors, puttering in her garden next door. Maddox had learned all their names during the fire incident, but had promptly forgotten them. This might be Lucy? Or Trudy? Possibly Betty.

"You don't know where Verity is, do you?" he asked hopefully.

The old woman shook her head, and Maddox's heart sank. But then she pointed down the street. "Can't tell you where she is now, but I saw her head out thataway a little while back. Looked like she was going downtown, maybe."

Hmmm. Maddox heaved himself up off the steps and set off to look for other Verity sightings.

Nearly everyone in town seemed to know her; she was fairly distinctive with her long skirts and long hair and the white cane she carried when she was out and about, and most people had gone into her tea shop at some point or another.

"Oh, the tea lady!" said a young woman pushing a little girl on a swing. "Yes, I saw her walking down by Tanner's Market this morning."

"No, she didn't come in here," said the clerk at Tanner's Market, a young man with a scraggly mustache. "But I saw her across the street, heading toward the park."

And so on, and so forth, until he ended up in the county records office talking to the woman behind the counter, cheerful and friendly with a head of piled-up curls.

"Oh yes, her! I helped her look through the city bylaws and other records, until she found what I guess she was looking for. She had me print it out for her."

"Print out what?" Maddox asked.

"The city charter. Here, you can look too if you like."

Maddox looked, but it might as well be gibberish to him. Just a bunch of legal mumbling about the boundaries of the town and so forth.

"Any idea why she wanted this?" he asked.

"I don't know, but she had me run off a copy and then asked if I could call a taxi to take her to the county seat."

"Why?"

"No idea. She seemed really excited, though."

There was only one possibility he could think of. "The county seat—does Ducker have an office there?"

"Well, I guess he does. Want me to find the address?"

"Yeah." His voice was so harsh that the secretary drew back from it. Maddox forced himself to calm down, lower his voice, hunch his shoulders to appear less big—all the little tricks he'd picked up over the years to make himself less scary when he needed to. "I mean, please do that."

He struggled to get control of himself. Losing his cool and scaring the secretary wouldn't help anyone, least of all Verity. But all signs pointed to Verity having found something that she thought could save the town, and she'd run off to confront Ducker with it.

"Yes, here it is, right in the middle of downtown," the secretary said, running a finger across a page of the old-school phone book in front of her.

"How do I get there? Too far to walk?"

"There's a bus that runs a few times a day. Or I could call you a cab. It might take awhile; there's only one cab in town."

"Yeah. Do that. Please."

As he left the building, he tried once again to call Verity. His call went to voice mail. This time, he stopped himself from hanging up.

"Verity, it's me. Maddox. I, uh, please don't do anything stupid 'til I can find you."

Okay, that was a terrible message, he thought as he closed the connection. He should have told her to call him. Maybe she'd think of it on her own when she got the message.

Maybe it was already too late.

He hesitated with his phone in hand. He could go ahead and call the FBI, like Loretta had suggested. It was probably a good idea ... for someone else.

But now his mate was in danger, and getting the proper authorities involved would only guarantee that he'd be shut out of helping her, forced to sit on the sidelines while they went endlessly through official channels and anything could be happening to Verity. His hands would be tied. He wouldn't have the option of contacting Darius for backup either, not without turning a glaring official eye on Darius and Loretta.

So much for doing things the right way. In the end, it always seemed to come down to doing things *his* way.

≈

D ucker's office was in a big fancy high-rise building. Just looking at it made Maddox's blood pressure skyrocket. The guy already had so much. Why did he want more so badly that he had to chase honest working people off their land?

"Mr. Ducker isn't here," the receptionist told him. "Do you have an appointment?"

"I think he'll want to talk to me. It's about Verity Breslin."

"Sir, that name means nothing to me." But her gaze flickered away from his eyes. Maddox had seen people do that before when they were lying. She slipped a hand under the desk. "You'll have to leave or I'm going to call security."

Maddox leaned on the desk, heavily enough that it creaked under his weight. "See, lady, I think you're lying. I think he's in here, and I'm not leaving 'til I see him."

"She's not lying."

Maddox glanced around quickly. Sheriff Hawkins stood just inside the door to the office, regarding him levelly. Maddox braced himself for a fight, but the sheriff merely tilted his head at him. "Come with me if you want to see your girlfriend."

Maddox's bull reared up inside him. It was all he could do to keep a grip on his temper, and on his animal. *It's for Verity,* he told himself. He wasn't still that person who used to solve all his problems with his fists. Not anymore. But if they'd hurt her, nothing on Earth could save them.

"What did you do?" he asked coldly as he followed Hawkins out the door. "Where is she?"

"She's not hurt. Not yet."

Maddox's hands curled into massive fists. He wished he had them around Hawkins' thick neck. "If there's a scratch on her, I'll break every bone in your body. Where *is* she?"

Hawkins glanced sideways at him. "I think I'm done taking orders from Ducker. I want to flip on him. Take what I know to the authorities. I want to know you won't come after me if I do that."

"I don't give a damn what you do. I don't care what Ducker does either. I just want to know where my mate is."

Hawkins blew out a breath. "She's at an old silver mine north of town. I can tell you how to get there. Hell ... I can drive you. But Ducker's still out there, and he's got a bunch of other guys with him. You'll have to fight your way through a small army to get to her."

Let me at 'em, Maddox's bull responded.

"Not you, though?" Maddox said.

"I told him I had business in town." Hawkins grimaced. "I haven't told him about you, about your ... animal, by the way."

"I'm not gonna thank you."

"Didn't expect you to."

Hawkins' sheriff's cruiser was parked by the curb. Hawkins opened the door and gave Maddox a look. He circled around and got into the passenger side in front. It was the first time he'd ever been in a cop car without cuffs on.

"Why are you doing this, anyway?" he asked Hawkins as the sheriff slid behind the wheel. "Don't expect me to believe you had a sudden attack of conscience."

Hawkins shook his head. "It's not that, not exactly. Let's just say I've been thinking about what you said. You said some things that made me take a look at my life in a whole new way. You're right, this isn't the life I wanted for me or my family. I don't know if it's possible to start over, but I want to try."

There were a lot of things Maddox could have said to that, but he found himself thinking about his own life. About the way Darius had given him a chance after he got out of prison—and the way he'd walked away from Darius eventually, to try to be his own man out from under the heavy hand of the dragon clanlord.

"Sometimes it is," he said slowly. "If you're willing to put in the work. And ..." He gestured to his own bad leg. "Willing to take your lumps, too."

"Guess we'll find out." Hawkins threw the car in gear. "Let's go get your girl."

VERITY

Verity had tried, at first, to keep track of the twists and turns where they'd taken her, but she eventually gave up. Now she was someplace quiet, and she had no idea where.

At some point she'd been handed off from Hawkins to some of Ducker's other hirelings. She'd never expected to miss the asshole sheriff, but at least he hadn't been manhandling her so roughly. These guys were abusive and crude and had ended up carrying her when she refused to walk, only to throw her to the sand in a place that echoed.

They walked away, and she heard the distant *thunk* of something heavy falling into place. She felt her way after them, groping along a cave wall until her fingers touched wooden timbers. She felt it all over, some kind of heavy door, blocking her way.

They had shut her up in an old mine and then left her.

She sat down on the sand and took slow, deep breaths until she felt calmer.

No one is every going to find you, Ducker had said.

But he was wrong. Maddox would. She was absolutely certain of that.

MADDOX

I t was starting to get dark when Hawkins pulled over and stopped. They'd been driving down an old dirt road for awhile, passing no other cars, although deep tire marks indicated that more than one vehicle had been on the road before them.

"The mine's up ahead," Hawkins said. "I can't take you closer without being seen. You know this is a trap, right? They expect you're going to show up to try to rescue her."

"I'm counting on it," Maddox said. He checked for cell service and wasn't surprised to get none; there would be no calling for help. "Hey, don't suppose you could back me up a little while longer. I could use the help."

Hawkins drummed thick fingers on the steering wheel. "Ducker knows where my family is. I'm not going against him head-on, not without protection for them."

"I get that," Maddox said. "Appreciate what you've done so far."

He opened his door. Night air, lightly scented with the fragrant smells of the desert, swept into the cab of the cruiser. Maddox started to step down to the shoulder of the road, then turned back.

"Hey, sheriff, if you'd do me one more thing?"

He scribbled Darius's number on the back of a receipt from the glove box and handed it to Hawkins. "When you get back to town, call this number and tell him where I am. Where we are. You don't have to give him your name, but if you want to, he can protect you better than a whole armed division of feds." If Darius didn't just decide to bite him in half, but Maddox chose not to mention that part.

"Who is he?" Hawkins asked, fingering the receipt.

"My old boss. A much bigger and meaner boss than yours."

Hawkins didn't say anything, but he tucked the receipt into his shirt pocket. Maddox slammed the door and stepped back so Hawkins could pull out onto the road. As the cruiser's taillights faded into the dusk, he turned and left the road, heading into the brush.

It wasn't fully dark yet, but it was getting there fast. Distant coyotes yipped in the night. Closer to Maddox, the scrub rustled softly with the sounds of little night creatures going about their business.

He leaned heavily on his cane, his hip aching. He'd given it a real workout already, and the night was far from done. About halfway up the hill, he decided that he needed more than two legs if he wasn't going to be completely useless by the time he got to the mine. He took off his clothes, bundled them up, and stashed them under a rock. He could come back for them later.

Hopefully he'd still have need of them.

The night seemed less dark and much warmer after he shifted, full of interesting smells. Taking the weight off his back leg, supporting his bulk on the other three legs, helped a lot with the ache in his hip. Maddox sniffed the air, snorted, and began to climb, still limping but not as severely as before.

He reached the top of the hill and looked down into a small valley. There were several cars and trucks, with their headlights lighting up the timbers of the old mine entrance. Ducker was visible by the glimmer of his silver hair, talking to a couple of men with guns slung over their shoulders. Maddox estimated about a half dozen others around the vehicles.

His bull's sharper-than-human senses of smell and hearing also alerted him to the presence of a sentry nearby, stationed atop the hill. Maddox moved toward the source of the people-smell carefully, his bull's massive hooves crunching on the gravel.

"What the hell—?" The sentry swung an automatic rifle toward him and then lowered it with a groan as Maddox took a bite of the nearest tasty-smelling bush. "Jeez. Just some stray cow."

As soon as he turned away again, Maddox shifted and moved in quickly behind him on bare feet to grab him from behind in a chokehold. The guard went down and Maddox stole his rifle, along with his boots to reduce the risk of stepping on a cactus or a rattlesnake. Wearing boots and nothing else, he went down the hill quietly toward the mouth of the mine, staying to the shadows.

Distraction. He needed a distraction. After thinking for a moment, he crouched behind a rock and set up the automatic rifle pointing across the valley. He hooked a bootlace around the trigger and carefully bent over a bush and tied the end of the lace loosely to hold the bush in place. It would snap back in moments, pulling the trigger.

Maddox kicked off the ill-fitting boots and shifted back to his bull. He trotted down the hill, making no particular effort to hide. Everything depended now on whether he could trust Hawkins. If Hawkins had told the truth about keeping Maddox's secret, if Hawkins hadn't tipped off Ducker that he was coming here tonight. Maddox wasn't normally a leap-of-faith kind of guy. Maybe Verity had rubbed off on him.

Or maybe it was just that he didn't have a choice. His mate was in danger. He had to get close to her, no matter the risk.

Several rifles swung toward him as he wandered into the pool of headlights, stopping and starting, trying to do his best impression of some farmer's strayed prize bull.

"Holy shit, look at the size of that cow," someone said.

I'm not a cow, Maddox's bull protested grumpily.

Knock it off, ya big ox.

"Anyone in the mood for beef tonight?" someone said, and there was scattered laughter.

Maddox scuffed the ground with a hoof and nibbled at a bush, but he had no appetite. They might shoot him even if they didn't know who he really was. He wouldn't put it past them. Ducker stood back, looking amused. There was blood at the corner of his mouth, and he occasionally dabbed at it with a handkerchief. *I bet Verity did that,* Maddox thought proudly. That was his mate, all right.

"You see a brand on this big guy?" one of the gunmen asked.

Maddox's bull reacted in horror at the idea of being branded. Maddox merely snorted in bovine laughter. Let them try.

His distraction better come soon, before they *did* try.

He was braced for it, but it still made him jump when it happened, a chattering burst of gunfire from high on the hillside as his twig-trap finally snapped.

The reactions were immediate, men flinging themselves

behind cars and spinning around to see where it was coming from.

And Maddox burst into motion. His hooves shook the ground as he galloped through the men, headed toward the opening to the mine.

No one tried to stop him. Why would they? He was an animal seeking refuge from a loud noise—a large, extremely difficult-to-stop animal, no less. Instead Ducker's gunmen threw themselves out of the way, and he reached the entrance to the mine without interference.

He encountered a new problem here. The mine entrance was too narrow for him to easily enter with his huge body. He thought the shaft would probably accommodate him, but he had to tilt his head to the side and dip it uncomfortably toward the ground to get his horns inside. He forced his way forward, feeling the door timbers scraping his massive shoulders.

"That is one seriously spooked cow," someone said behind him.

Bull, his animal protested.

Maddox had other things on his mind than defending his bull's honor. His nostrils flared at the smell of his mate. Verity was in here somewhere.

He pushed his way forward, wincing as his horns snagged at the ceiling and walls even with his head tilted forward and down at a neck-straining angle. It was so dark he couldn't see, especially with his head twisted to the side. But the darkness was good, he thought as he pushed ever deeper into the mine. He couldn't look back to see if he was being followed, but as soon as he was deep enough that the darkness would cloak him from onlookers, he could shift back to a shape more practical for navigating mines.

Before he could do that, however, he ran into another of

Ducker's guards—almost literally. Already spooked from the sound of gunfire and shouting outside, the guard shone a flashlight in his face and then let out a shocked yell. Maddox was dimly aware of movement behind the light, knew there was going to be a gun involved, and lunged forward, head-butting the man to the ground with his bony bovine forehead. Then he shifted in mid-stride and punched the dazed guard in the face.

He retrieved the man's rifle just as another guard appeared in the tunnel up ahead. The sight of a naked man standing over his colleague gave him just enough pause for Maddox to get in the first shot. The man went down without a sound.

Lowering the weapon, Maddox looked up nervously as sand sifted down from the ceiling at the concussion of the gunshots. The whole mine was probably unstable. *Gotta be careful. Don't want to bring it down on us.*

Then he heard the sweetest sound in the world—Verity's voice, muffled, calling from further down the tunnel, "Who's out there?"

"It's me!" Maddox shouted back.

Snatching up a flashlight, with the guard's rifle bouncing against his bare side, he hurried toward the sound of her voice. A heavy wooden door soon blocked his path. Made of thick, weathered timbers, it didn't block the way entirely. There were narrow gaps at the sides where the timbers had warped and the ill-fitting door had been hammered into place. Through one of these gaps, Verity's dirt-smudged fingers flickered pale in the flashlight's beam. Maddox met her hand with his own, and they twined their fingers together, unable to get closer.

"You found me." Her voice was relieved, but not panicked. "I knew you would."

"I'll always find you. No matter what."

She gave a choked laugh. "That would sound so cheesy coming from someone else, but you make me believe it."

"Always." He glanced over his shoulder. That gunfire would bring pursuit, as soon as they got past the fear of encountering an enraged bull in extremely close quarters. "Stand back. I'm going to try to push this out of the way."

"Can you?" Verity asked. Her voice retreated as she backed off.

"I don't know. Get well back. I'm going to try to move it just enough to break the bolts holding it in place, but I don't know what'll happen."

"Be careful," Verity said, her voice more distant now.

Maddox shifted, and let out a snort of pain as his body bulked out in the close confines of the tunnel and his horns dug painfully into the compacted dirt of the shaft. It was even narrower here than closer to the entrance; he could barely move. But that was a help. It gave him better traction to push.

He lowered his head and pressed his forehead into the door, then bore down with all the strength of his great body.

Nails shrieked. The door shifted in its frame. Dust sifted down, powdering his hide and getting in his eyes.

"Maddox, stop!" Verity cried. "You're going to bring the tunnel down!"

He paused his efforts and stood still for a moment, his flanks heaving as dust continued to sift down and things creaked and groaned ominously around him. While he held still, the unnerving creaking stopped as the tunnel settled into its new configuration.

"It's not worth it, Maddox," Verity called through the door. "We can find another way."

He shifted back, gasping in relief when the tunnel was no longer pressing on his shoulders and horns. "I might be able to pivot the door enough now that you can get out. But we've still got a problem back there. Ducker's outside, and he's got hired guns with him."

"Can you get in here with me? Hide until they go away? There might be a back way out."

Maddox pushed at the edge of the door, dislodged slightly in its frame, but still securely wedged in place. It scraped a few more inches and then refused to move any further. "I'm not sure—"

Boots pounded in the tunnel behind him. He turned around, putting himself between Verity and the men who had just appeared with flashlight beams dancing and jumping as they ran.

Maddox snatched up the rifle and leveled it at them, squinting against the lights. At his feet, the stolen flashlight lay where he'd dropped it, pointed at the wall and haloing him in a dim pool of light. "You want to do this? If I go down, some of you are going with me. Is he paying you enough for this?"

"Where the hell did *you* come from?" Ducker's voice demanded. Maddox couldn't tell which one he was, behind the glaring flashlights. "And why the hell are you naked?"

"Surprising how easy you and your boys are to distract," Maddox said. Behind him, he heard scrabbling as Verity struggled to pivot the door further and enlarge the gap. "I'd look behind you, if I were you."

"Maddox, it's not moving!" Verity whispered loudly.

"Get back," he whispered. Taking a deep breath, he dropped the gun and kicked the flashlight with one bare foot. In a dancing whirl of shadows, he shifted.

From the viewpoint of the men in the corridor, the bull must have exploded out of nowhere. Maddox lashed out behind him with his powerful hind feet, and felt the door give. There were yells of shock, and gunfire erupted as he shifted again. He tumbled backward and fell through the gap between the door and the wall. A bullet burned across his ribs, another across his thigh. The sharp edge of the door scraped his shoulder painfully.

Verity caught him, pulling him along with her. More bullets splintered the wood of the door, but Maddox and Verity stumbled up the tunnel, shielded from view. Although askew, the door still blocked most of the corridor behind them.

He hadn't been able to grab the flashlight. They were in total darkness now, lit only by the gleam of flashlights from somewhere beyond the door. Light shone through the holes and through the gap between the door and the wall. His kick had swung it a couple of feet, enough to create a big enough gap for one man to get through.

"Stay down," Maddox murmured. He put himself between Verity and the door. "If they come, they'll have to come single file."

"Are you hurt?" she whispered.

"Not bad," he whispered back, trying to ignore the trickle of blood down his leg.

Now that the gunfire had died away, there was silence from the other side of the door, broken only by occasional, ominous groaning from the ceiling. Maddox was acutely aware of the countless tons of rock and dirt above them. Sweat ran down his face and tickled the small of his back. Give him an honest fistfight any day; he'd gladly take that over this trapped feeling, especially with his mate's life at stake too.

"Where did the damn thing go?" he heard Ducker shouting from behind the door. "Never mind! If it's in there with them, I hope they enjoy themselves." There was a murmured discussion too distant to make out, and then Ducker called, "Mr. Murphy! Are you listening?"

Maddox didn't respond. He could hear Verity's sharp, quick breaths behind him.

"Very well, if that's how you want it. Goodbye, Mr. Murphy."

And then there were no more voices. Flashlight beams flickered behind the door, and then everything was still and quiet, lit with a faint glow.

A trap? It had to be. They'd left men behind, surely.

The ceiling groaned again. More gravel pattered down, and Verity gave a little gasp. Trap or not, they couldn't stay here.

"Wait for me," he murmured, and crept forward on bare feet until he could peek around the edge of the door.

The men were gone, but what they'd left behind made his blood run cold.

Dynamite. Hissing and spitting as its fuse burned down.

He turned and sprinted back to Verity. "Go, go, go!" No time for stealth now. Their only hope was to put as much distance between themselves and the explosion as possible, and hope it didn't bring the entire cave system down.

"What's going on?" Verity gasped as he pulled her along, stumbling over rocks and fallen timbers.

"They've got the place rigged to explode." Any second now. "Down, down!"

Maddox pushed her down as gently as possible and threw himself over her. He bulked out into the mass of his bull with knees bent on either side of Verity's suddenly small and fragile body, bowed his head and felt her arms come up around his neck. *Don't*, he wanted to tell her—she had to stay beneath him, let him cover as much of her as possible. But she wrapped her arms around his neck and pressed her face into his hide, and then the tunnel shook under them and rocks came down on them in a lethal rain.

VERITY

"Maddox?" Verity managed to get the word out through a coughing fit. The air was full of dust, thick and choking.

The noise had finally died away, the shuddering and tremendous sense of motion around her had ceased, and there was still space beneath Maddox's neck for her to breathe. To her vast relief, she could feel the slow, heavy beating of his heart, vibrating through the great chest trapping her legs.

"Maddox!" She gave him a sharp shake, and heard the rattling of pebbles around her. "Maddox, wake up. You're crushing my legs."

Maddox groaned faintly, and then the great bulk her arms were wrapped around suddenly dwindled to smooth human skin. Verity let out a startled cry as rocks and dirt shifted all around them, pushing on their bodies. But they weren't completely buried; they couldn't be, because she could still breathe.

"Maddox?"

"Verity," he murmured. His hand brushed the side of her head, then found its way to her face. "You okay?"

"I'm not hurt. Not badly." Though a long way from *okay*; she had a feeling they both were.

"Can't see a damn thing. It's dark as a tomb in here." Then a huff of a laugh tickled her neck. "Guess that's nothing you aren't used to, though."

She couldn't help but smile. "Yeah, for me it's nothing unusual." She felt along his bare back until her hand encountered dirt and rocks. "How buried are we?"

"Can't tell. Can you move?"

Together they struggled to push the rocks away from their legs until they could crawl on top of what felt to Verity like a loose and unstable mass of dirt and rocks and splintered timbers. She reached above her head and touched wood, then felt her way along a beam that had bent in the middle, with sharp-edged cracks running through it. Although she touched it very lightly, she felt a faint shudder run through it, and heard groaning in the walls around them that chilled her soul.

"I think we should get away from here. This whole part of the tunnel might collapse."

"Can't even tell which way we came from. Can you?"

Verity could, but she had a bad feeling it didn't matter: the tunnel behind them was almost certainly blocked. She confirmed it by feeling her way over the rocks and dirt. In one direction, it filled the tunnel all the way to the ceiling. The other way, deeper into the mine, was the only possibility.

"Come on." She took his big hand in hers. His fingers were cold, reminding her of the feeling of his bare body pressed against hers a few moments earlier. "Where are your clothes?"

"Outside. Guess I'll just have to deal."

179

Hand in hand, they felt their way over and among the loose rocks half-blocking the tunnel. "Careful," Verity murmured. Even through her shoes, she could tell there were broken boards, sharp rocks, and possibly rusty nails in the mix of debris underfoot.

The going got easier as they made their way farther up the tunnel, with the floor mostly clear and solid underfoot. Still, Verity slowed down even more here, realizing that there could be any kind of dangers up ahead, including vertical shafts they wouldn't know about until they fell down one.

"Something wrong?" Maddox asked quietly.

"Just worried about stepping on something in the dark. Can you see at all?"

There was a whisper of sound that might have been Maddox shaking his head. "Dark as the inside of a black cat."

"See if you can find anything we can use to feel out the path ahead, like a loose board or a stick."

They eventually found what felt like a pile of loose boards, warped and tinder-dry after lying in the mine for unknown decades. Verity found one that was slim and light enough that she could swing it in front of her. She guided Maddox's hand to the pile of boards, and he picked up a bigger, heavier one.

"You go ahead and guide both of us. You're better at this. I'll just keep hold of your hand and leave my other hand free for defending us if I have to."

"Sounds like a deal," she said, forcing a smile until remembering that he couldn't see it in the dark. "We're a heck of a team, huh?"

"Yeah, we are." He leaned close to her and kissed ... well, the top of her ear, but he was probably aiming for her cheek, and then he put an arm around her and just held her for a moment. "Verity, I'm so sorry I left. So sorry I scared you. Sorry about Ducker and—"

"Okay, you just stop right there. I got myself in trouble with Ducker all on my own. There are more than enough bad decisions to go around here."

"Fair enough," he agreed. "But I promise I'll never leave again. Not for any reason."

"I'm going to hold you to that," she told him, and tilted her head back for a kiss.

～

Verity led them through the dark, moving slowly, feeling her way ahead with the board. Maddox was limping heavily; she could tell by the way he jerked at every step, his fingers tugging at hers.

"How are you doing?" she asked quietly. "Do you need to stop?" It was chilly down here; he must be cold, aside from possibly being more badly hurt than he wanted to admit.

"I'm fine," he said, and she had to take his word for it. They didn't really have any other options.

She had thought it would be utterly silent underground, and was surprised to find that it was not, though it had seemed that way to her when Ducker had first left her in the mine. But the longer she was down here, the more she became aware of other sounds, echoing strangely in the network of tunnels. Faint creaking and groaning in the walls —but not close, she didn't think. Rattles and plops of falling rocks, dripping water; at first she mistook it for footsteps, but after awhile she came to accept it as part of the background music of the caves.

She was very surprised to find that she liked it down here. In fact, once they got back to the surface (she refused to consider that they might not) she thought about asking Bailey to look into local caving opportunities and find out if there were any guided tours and whether she might be able to learn how to do it herself.

Would caving be an appropriate hobby for a blind woman? *Well, I'd save a bunch on headlamp batteries,* she thought, and smiled to herself.

They went through a number of junctions and branches in the tunnels. Verity paused to mark each of these with a stone placed in the middle of the tunnel; hopefully it would be enough to allow them to backtrack if they had to. They came to a couple of dead ends and had to go back and try the other way, but the tunnel network seemed to go on and on, never ending.

"There *must* be another way out," Verity told Maddox, pausing to pick up some more rocks for tunnel-marking. She put them in the pocket of her skirt. "Surely it wouldn't make sense to have just one way in and out of the mine."

"I don't see why not."

"But it's inefficient, especially if you're mining close to the surface. If you have more entrances, you can get more people in, and take more material out." She hesitated, listening to the sound of Maddox's heavy breathing. "Should we stop for a few minutes?"

"I just want to get out of here."

She had assumed his issues were physical; now she began to wonder if the problem was more psychological. "Is it bothering you, being down here?"

"Bothering me?" He gave a short laugh. "Isn't it bothering *you?*"

"Not really. I mean, I want to get *out,* of course. But I'm sure there's a way. I'm not naked, though," she felt compelled to add.

"I just can't stop thinking about how far down we are. I never thought tight spaces bothered me, but this—! And it's so damn dark. Of course I know how it sounds, me complaining about that, it must annoy you—"

"No, of course not. I'm used to it, but it must be very hard to cope with if you're used to using your eyes to find your way around."

"It feels like the dark is pressing on my eyes. I can't even tell if they're open or closed."

She squeezed his hand. "Focus on the other things you can feel from your body. The ground under your feet. The ..."

Wind on her face?

"Maddox, do you feel that?" She turned her head, trying to recapture the slight breeze that had stirred her hair. "I think it was a draft. Some kind of air movement."

They started walking again with renewed energy, and soon she was certain. When they came to the next branch in the tunnel, she was able to choose by holding a hand in front of each option. There was definitely air movement in the tunnel they were now in, and the air smelled fresher.

"I'll be damned." There was a hoarseness to Maddox's voice that worried her, but he sounded more energized. "You were right. There *is* a way out."

"Let's not get too excited. It might just be a ventilation shaft."

But it wasn't. She could smell juniper and creosote brush. She began to hurry, but Maddox caught her arm and pulled her to a halt.

"What?" she said, but he touched a finger to her lips and she hushed.

"There's definitely an opening up there. I can see the stars." Wonder, for a moment, filled his whispering voice. "But they might've posted a guard on the exits. It's what I would've done. You stay here while I go scout ahead."

Despite what she'd said about not minding being underground, everything in her now yearned to get out of the confines of the tunnel walls and feel the night wind on her face again. But she could see his point. "Okay, just hurry. I'll wait here."

Maddox squeezed her hand, and his quiet footsteps, hitching with a profound limp, receded from her.

MADDOX

F ree! He'd never been so glad to see the stars overhead or feel the night breeze on his chilled body. It was all he could do not to throw himself through the cave mouth and run laughing down the hillside.

But he didn't—for a number of reasons, including the fact that stepping on a rattlesnake with his bare feet wasn't going to improve his night.

Instead, he pressed himself to the wall just inside the entrance and listened carefully. He heard the sounds of the night, small rustlings and a distant coyote howling and somewhere a far-off car on an unseen road.

He hadn't expected being trapped underground to affect him so profoundly. He wasn't claustrophobic, at least not that he'd ever noticed. But it was such an incredibly helpless feeling, knowing that he couldn't get out, couldn't even shift into his bull in some of the narrow places they'd gone through. And the *darkness*. He knew it didn't bother Verity because she was used to it, but he'd found himself getting jumpier and jumpier, never knowing what direction danger might be coming from.

He'd far rather confront his enemies head-on.

And it was time to do just that—assuming they were here. Maddox picked up a pebble, weighed it in his palm, then tossed it out the cave mouth into the fragrant desert night. It skittered among the bushes.

There was no obvious reaction, but he heard soft rustling off to the right, as of someone readjusting themselves.

Damn. Sometimes he hated being right.

He glanced back to where he'd left Verity; his dark-adapted eyes caught a glimpse of her face and the glimmer of the white patches on her skirt. Looked like she was staying put. At least that was one thing he didn't have to worry about. He crept to the cave entrance and for a moment he stayed there, marshaling his strength. He was exhausted and cold; his feet hurt, his hip hurt, and blood had dried to sticky crusts on his flank and thigh. All he wanted to do was lie down for a week.

You can rest when your mate is safe, he told himself. He lunged out of the cave, shifting as he went.

The sight of a bull erupting from the cave mouth was enough of a distraction that when someone else's gun went off near him, he was already past where they expected him to be. There appeared to be only one sentry, and Maddox kicked him in the chest, sending him tumbling down the hill. There was a yelp and a series of painful-sounding thumps.

Maddox shifted back and dropped to a crouch, just as gunfire sprayed through the brush, coming from somewhere farther up the hill.

Maddox ducked behind a boulder. The shooting stopped, and he heard someone say somewhere, not too far away, "Where the hell did that thing *go*? It's too big to just disappear!"

"Forget about the damn cow," Ducker's voice said. "That

could've been a distraction. Does anyone see Murphy around anywhere?"

Static crackled from further down the hill, where the guard had landed in a tangle of brush. The other voice said, "Jim's not answering his radio."

"Dammit," Ducker snapped, and called, "Mr. Murphy? Are you there?"

Maddox didn't answer.

"You *are* resourceful. I thought for sure the cave-in would have taken care of you. Remember that job offer? It's still open."

"I wouldn't work for you if you held a gun to my head," Maddox called back.

"Ah, but what if I held a gun to *her* head?"

Sheer panic almost made him spring to his feet—probably with lethal results. But then his conscious mind got the better of his fear for Verity. He hadn't heard anything from the cave. She *must* still be in there. Ducker was bluffing.

Two could play that game.

"She's dead!" he called back. "I got out of your cave-in. She didn't."

"Then it's just you, a man alone. You won't escape, you know. You're badly outnumbered."

Maddox glanced down the hill. Flashlights swept back and forth: more of Ducker's people, closing in on him. He might be able to make a run for it as a bull, but that would mean abandoning Verity. He'd rather die.

But if they think she's already dead ...

"How about I surrender," he called. "We can discuss that job offer over beers, somewhere warm."

"Throw your weapons away and stand up."

Maddox stood up, hands raised. "I'm not armed."

"I still wonder what happened to your clothes," Ducker

remarked. He came strolling down the hillside above the cave. He wasn't armed; he didn't need to be. The gunmen on either side of him took care of that.

Maddox forced himself not to look at the cave, not even to *think* about the cave for fear of giving himself away. *Just stay out of sight, Verity, no matter what you hear.*

"It's a really long story," he said. It went against every instinct to keep himself still, not to try to fight or resist. "Let's have a cold one and talk about it."

"Or I could shoot you where you stand," Ducker said calmly.

"Maddox! No!"

Damn it.

Verity appeared in the entrance to the cave, clutching the board like a baseball bat: a furious avenging angel, incensed on his behalf. "Leave him alone!" she shouted, to the night in general since she had no idea which way to look.

Maddox lunged toward her, expecting at any moment to feel the impact of a bullet, but nothing happened. He landed barefoot next to her. When he put a hand on her arm, she whipped around and swung the board at his head. Maddox caught it with shifter-fast reflexes.

"Verity, it's me!"

"Oh," she gasped, and dropped the board, putting her arms around him.

"You could have been safe," he told her, moving to put his body between her and the approaching gunmen. "All you had to do was wait in the cave 'til we were gone."

Her answer was quiet, pitched for his ears alone. "There is no safety for me without you."

"Charming," Ducker remarked. His squeaky-new cowboy boots skidded down the last little slope; he stumbled and one of his men had to steady him. Then he appraised them from a few yards off, his thumbs tucked into his belt. "What a charming scene. I really don't know what to do with you two. I've made every offer to resolve this peacefully."

Maddox couldn't help snorting with bitter laughter, and Verity snapped, "Like setting my shop on fire and throwing dynamite at us? If that's your idea of a peaceful solution, I'd hate to see what you consider a violent one!"

Ducker looked more entertained than upset, as if he was amused by a kitten hissing and snarling at him. Maddox had an urge to turn Verity loose on him with her board. She'd change his mind pretty quick.

... and also get herself shot.

Which was likely to happen to them both in the next few minutes. Maddox had no illusion that Ducker planned to let them go. It made all the sense in the world that he wouldn't. They both posed a threat to him in different ways, and he was never going to get a better opportunity to get rid of both of them with no one the wiser.

They weren't both getting out of here—but, Maddox thought, maybe he could get Verity out. If he shifted quickly, blocking the entrance to the cave ... he wouldn't last long, but she could run deep into the tunnels and hide. She was good enough at navigating down there that she might be able to escape a search and come back up when it was safe. It wasn't a good plan, but it was the only one he had.

"Verity," he said softly. "Listen, when I start moving—"

"Don't you dare suggest sacrificing yourself for me," Verity snapped back. "Did you miss everything I said earlier? Or the part where your life wouldn't even be in danger if not for me?"

"I don't want a life without you in it."

"Touching," Ducker remarked. He gestured to his men. Maddox held Verity and kept himself between the gunmen and her. Even if she wouldn't leave him, he could at least protect her for a little while by shifting, and maybe take some of them with him too. It was possible that once he was dead, they'd have second thoughts about killing an unarmed blind woman.

"I'm sorry," Verity whispered.

"I'm not," he whispered back, and got ready to shift. If he was going down, he meant to go down fighting.

But nothing happened. Instead, Ducker was looking around, and so were some of his men. Verity tilted her head as if she was listening. And then Maddox heard something too, a strangely out of place sound out here in the middle of nowhere. Some kind of engine noise, deep and low, shivering the ground under his feet—

The helicopter came skimming over the top of the hill, its rotor-and-engine noise suddenly deafening, along with a brilliant light that stabbed down at them and froze Ducker and his men where they stood. The helicopter circled above them, and a voice on a loudspeaker announced, "This is the FBI. Lay down your weapons and put your hands on your head."

"What on Earth?" Verity gasped, her arms tightening around Maddox in a convulsive clasp.

A second helicopter was coming in from the other direction, and Ducker's men started dropping their guns; they weren't getting paid enough to get in a shootout with the police. Ducker stepped back, his mouth tight, and folded his hands over the top of his wind-whipped gray hair. "This'll never stick," he snapped over the roar of the helicopter above them. "I have the best law firm in this state on retainer. I'll be out by this afternoon and I'm coming for you, Murphy. You *and* your woman."

"You know what?" Maddox said, his eyes tracking the second helicopter. It had lowered to hover above the rocks of the hillside, and a door in the side slid open so that a tall, graceful figure, dressed in a black suit, could jump out to land gracefully beneath the whipping rotors. "I really don't think that's going to happen."

The second helicopter lifted off again, and Darius Keegan strolled across the hillside, through the surrendering gunmen, looking completely unconcerned, carrying a canvas shopping bag with a bright orange cartoon cat on it. He passed Ducker without even bothering to look at him, to Ducker's spluttering indignation, and stopped in front of Maddox and Verity.

Maddox hadn't seen Darius in almost a year. The dragon shifter looked good—certainly better than when Maddox had last seen him, bruised and bandaged after fighting for his life. Now he looked tanned and healthy, holding his head high with all his old pride, though perhaps a little less swagger; it was a deep, casual confidence that Darius wielded these days. Loretta had been good for him.

With no hesitation, as if meeting naked former employees on a mountainside was an everyday occurrence for him, he opened the bag and held it out. "Your size," Darius said. "You might want to have pants on when you talk to the authorities."

"I'll bleed on it," Maddox said. Being confronted with Darius in his crisply tailored suit made him even more aware of his own bloody, filthy condition. Being naked hardly mattered; he was covered in such a layer of dirt and other filth that it hardly showed.

"Indeed," Darius said dryly, and gave the bag of clothes an impatient shake. "Because buying more cheap menswear is an expense I can barely afford. Put it on."

"How did you know he was going to need it?" Verity asked as Maddox leaned down stiffly to pull on a pair of pants. Now that the adrenaline was ebbing, his hip had locked up and all his various hurts were making themselves known in a major way.

"Let's just say that in a situation like this, people like us prefer to keep a spare set of clothing handy. Even if *my* kind doesn't have that problem."

Verity's sightless eyes flew wide. "You're—like him? No, wait." Verity was no fool. "You're the person he told me about. You're the—" She lowered her voice, though there was little chance of being overheard over the noise of the helicopters. "The *dragon*."

"Maddox," Darius said in a cool tone.

Maddox straightened up and buttoned the pair of brand-new jeans; he was unsurprised to discover they were a perfect fit. "She's my mate. I have no secrets from her."

"So I see." Darius didn't sound particularly upset about having his secret revealed—though with him, it was often hard to tell; he could be perfectly cool right up until the point when the claws came out. Maddox kept a wary eye on him, but it was with perfect politeness that he took Verity's hand and brought it to his lips, unconcerned about its filthy state. "A pleasure. I'm Darius."

"Verity Breslin." She drew her shoulders up and held herself proudly, and Maddox felt his heart swell and brim over with love for her. If it had been entirely up to him, he would have liked Darius's first sight of her to be sometime when she wasn't bedraggled and covered with dirt after being buried alive in a cave-in. But at the same time he realized Darius was actually seeing her at her best: proud and undaunted and brave and beautiful.

"You won't make this stick!" Ducker shouted, and Maddox looked around with the startled realization that he'd almost forgotten about his enemy. There were men and women in FBI jackets all over the hillside now, and Ducker had been slapped into handcuffs, which gave Maddox a deep satisfaction. "You can't *touch* me. I'll have all of your badges. As for you two—" He managed to cut himself off, apparently not yet far gone enough to threaten their lives in front of a bunch of FBI agents, but the look he gave Maddox and Verity promised retribution.

Darius leaned close and murmured, for their ears only, "You know, he *could* have a convenient little accident."

It was tempting—the idea of eliminating the threat to his mate, and to any future family they might have. Tempting. For just a moment. But that wasn't the kind of life he wanted to live. Not anymore.

And so Maddox shook his head firmly. "No. That's not me, not now. And it's not you either," he added, and saw from the look on Darius's face that he'd struck a nerve, especially when he went on, "I don't think Loretta would want you making offers like that anymore."

"True," Darius sighed regretfully. "Oh well." He watched Ducker being escorted to a helicopter in handcuffs. "Back in the time of my father, we would have gouged out his eyes, broken all his limbs, and cast him naked into our deepest caverns for daring to lay a hand on someone under the clan's protection."

"Yeah, that's kinda out of style these days."

"I suppose I'll just have to do this the human way, and drown him in lawyers. Spending the rest of his life in prison as his business empire is nibbled away by lawsuits ... that's a hell of its own sort, I suppose." He turned to Verity and took her hand again, guiding it to his arm. "And now, I expect you two would like to get out of here. The inevitable FBI questioning can take place in a more congenial location, if we hurry before they get any ideas."

Maddox retrieved Verity's hand from Darius's arm and placed it firmly on his own arm instead. Verity smiled, and her fingers tightened in a brief squeeze. "I think that sounds good. Especially if someone could pick us up a couple of burgers."

As they began walking back to Darius's helicopter, picking their way carefully across the rocky hillside, Darius smiled. "I think that could be arranged."

VERITY

For most of her life, Verity had rarely slept in. Even without the visual cues of sun and sky, she was usually up at dawn, bustling about her neatly kept kitchen to start her day.

So it was with a sense of disorientation that she drifted awake, unable to tell if it was early or late. The bed was soft and deep and unfamiliar. A hotel in Phoenix, she recalled, paid for by Maddox's friend Darius. They'd ended up here after giving the FBI endless repetitions of a carefully edited version of the past few weeks' events—true in all regards except that any bulls who appeared in the story must be stray cattle from nearby ranches and nothing else.

She felt her way past Maddox's sleeping warmth to the bedside table and her phone, thumbing down the volume so it wouldn't wake him when it told her the time. It was early evening; they'd slept the afternoon away, and she was hungry.

Maddox groaned beside her, and she felt him roll over. They were both finally, blessedly clean. After checking into the hotel, they'd showered and then fallen into bed, both of them exhausted and, for Verity's part, aching in muscles she hadn't even known she had. Maddox, she suspected, was worse off, not that he would admit it.

Her skin itself cringed from the idea of putting her filthy clothes back on to go out and get food. Maybe this was the kind of hotel that had room service, something she only knew about from books but had never actually experienced.

"Good morning, beautiful," Maddox murmured, his voice rough with sleep. Big, callused hands brushed her loose hair away from her face.

"Good morning yourself." She leaned into his kiss, and then the touch of his hands on her body. Eating, she decided, could wait for awhile.

An hour or so later, after another shower luxuriously shared under the hotel's ample hot water, they were up and about. Wrapped in fluffy bathrobes, they sat on the floor and Maddox read the hotel's room service menu aloud to her. She decided on pasta, and he had two of the largest steaks on the menu delivered to their room, along with a bottle of wine.

"Are you sure Darius won't mind?"

"He'll deal. He's not as loaded as he used to be, but he's still not poor. And I'm about to start gnawing on a chair leg."

"In that case, why don't you add some pie to that? If they have pie."

They did have pie, with ice cream, and she and Maddox were just licking the last of the vanilla ice cream off their spoons when there was a knock on the room door and a voice through the door said, "Aunt Verity?"

Verity jumped up to answer it, and the next thing she knew, she was being tightly hugged, bathrobe and all. "This is so wild!" Bailey exclaimed. "I've got a suitcase here with some of your clothes and stuff, by the way. Hi, Mr. Maddox!"

"Hi," Maddox said, from the floor.

"How did you know where to find us?" Verity asked. By the time they'd gotten out of the FBI's interrogation room, she had been so exhausted and overwhelmed that the idea of calling Bailey hadn't even occurred to her. And with her phone still missing—she expected Ducker had probably thrown it away—Bailey had no way to get in touch with her, either.

"One of Mr. Maddox's friends called us. He told us where you were, and we talked Luke's grandma into letting us drive down to pick you up and also bring you some things, since you had to go away so suddenly. Is Mr. Ducker really in *jail*?"

"Yes, he is. Do you want to hear the story?"

They ordered more food for the kids, and sat around on the floor and talked. Verity edited the story slightly to remove the most alarming parts, as well as all references to shifters, but Luke and Bailey hung on every word.

"So what happens now?" Bailey asked, her spoon clinking in her ice cream bowl. "Are they gonna, like, throw the book at them, or what?"

"You've been watching too many cop shows," Verity told her. "But, yes, Sheriff Hawkins is cutting a deal to testify against him." They had encountered him briefly at the FBI building, though they hadn't spoken to him; she'd recognized his voice down the hall, that was all.

"Is he going to come back and be sheriff again?" Luke asked, sounding unhappy with the prospect.

"I doubt it. I think his law-enforcement days are over, at least in Silvermine."

"Yay!" Bailey crowed. "This means Maddox can be our new sheriff!"

Maddox let out a snorted, startled laugh, and Verity said, "Bailey, that's up to Maddox, I think."

"But you're still running for sheriff, right?" the girl said. "If Mr. Hawkins is out of the race, then it's just you, and it's past the deadline so you *can't* withdraw, because that'd leave us without a sheriff at all and that would be really bad, right?"

"Bailey!" Verity said, smiling despite herself. But a coldness crept through her at the idea of Maddox leaving. He *could* leave now, she thought. If the threat to the town was over, was there anything to keep him around?

"Are you planning on leaving?" Bailey asked, the plaintiveness in her voice reflecting Verity's own thoughts.

Maddox's hand slid over Verity's, and he said quietly, "I think that's up to your Aunt Verity, if she wants me to stay or not."

"Of course I want you to stay!" Verity exclaimed, shocked. "Why *wouldn't* I want you to stay? Don't be ridiculous."

"Just didn't want to presume," Maddox said, but she could hear the smile in his voice.

Bailey's happy squeal was loud enough that Verity hushed her so they wouldn't bother the rest of the guests. Then there was a surprised huff from Maddox and Verity grinned at the mental image of the girl throwing her arms around him. He was, she thought, not a man who was used to being hugged.

"Uh, thanks," he said, as small shuffling noises indicated he was peeling Bailey off him. Verity braced herself, guessing what was coming, and she wasn't wrong, as her niece hugged her next.

"We should celebrate," Bailey declared. "Actually, we should go out and explore. Can we? Please? I know it's kinda late, but I've only been to Phoenix once on a band trip, and we didn't get to go *anywhere*."

"I can take 'em, if you want to stay here," Maddox told Verity.

"No," she said. "No, I think we should go out together. As a family. But let me get some clothes on first, okay? You kids go down and wait for us in the lobby. We'll be down soon."

"You better not get up to hanky-panky in here and make

us wait," Bailey declared, and then the door shut behind them.

Verity laughed and got up, feeling around for the suitcase Bailey had brought. Her heart clutched when she discovered that her niece had packed her suitcase in exactly the way she liked it, with everything compartmentalized neatly by clothing type, and had also brought her some toiletry things.

"She's such a sweet kid," she said to Maddox, sitting on the bed as she brushed out her hair.

"I know. They both are. There's just one problem," Maddox said with an embarrassed laugh. "I don't have a single dollar to my name. Not on me. Everything I had is under half a mountain right now."

Verity stood up and smoothed down her skirt, then held out her arm. "Let's just walk around, then. We just ate, so we don't have to eat again. We can just be tourists. If the kids want any souvenirs, they can buy them for themselves."

His arm slid smoothly under hers, as if it was meant to be there. "Will you enjoy it? Sightseeing? Though I guess it's not sightseeing for you, not exactly."

"I think I will." New smells, new places to explore—and somewhere to go back to, after all of it. Someone to support her, and guide her when she needed it, and stand by to catch her if she wanted to go it alone. The more she thought about it, the more excited she was to explore a city where she'd never been, despite living just a few hours' drive from it all her life. "I'm really looking forward to 'seeing' it."

As a family.

EPILOGUE

"Congratulations to the new sheriff!"

Maddox ducked his head, flattered and embarrassed. The patrons in the Whistlestop Café cheered, and cheered even more when the waitress brought free slices of warm strawberry pie, piled high with vanilla ice cream.

"Congratulations," she said warmly, passing pie around the table to Verity, Bailey, and Luke. "You'll be a *much* better sheriff than that other guy. I can tell already."

She left, and Maddox tried to pretend that his face wasn't as blazing hot as the desert sun, and probably as red as if he'd been hiking in the desert for days.

"I still can't believe people voted for me," he admitted, digging a fork into his pie. Verity squeezed his hand, and then found her own plate and fork with her fingertips.

"Well, you are the only candidate," Luke said from across the table in their booth. Bailey smacked him. "What? It's true!"

"You're gonna be a great sheriff, Maddox," Bailey declared

through a mouthful of pie. She and Luke had dug in with the appetites of active teenagers; their pie was half gone already.

"I don't even know how."

"We'll help you!" Bailey said. "Won't we, Aunt Verity?"

Verity smiled. "I think your first priority needs to be finishing your junior year and looking into colleges. *Then* we'll talk."

Bailey rolled her eyes and jammed her fork into her mouth with the last bite of pie. "Can Luke and I take his truck out to the lake this afternoon?"

"Yes, if you're back by sundown."

Bailey rose out of her seat and leaned across to kiss Verity's cheek, and then Maddox's, to his surprise. "Thanks! Love you guys!"

Luke made his polite goodbyes and then was off with Bailey dragging him by the hand, before Maddox could quite get over his shock. He knew Bailey liked him, and Verity had been clear that he was part of the family, but this was the first time she'd ever told him she loved him.

"At least these days, I can be confident they actually *are* going to the lake, instead of taking on the town's corrupt power structure single-handedly." Verity shook her head. "Though, come to think of it, I remember what we used to get up to at that lake when we were kids. Maybe they'd be better off chasing crooked city officials."

"You don't mean that."

"No," she said, her smile widening. "No, I don't. I'm so glad she's able to have a normal, carefree childhood at last. And the repairs on the shop are coming along nicely ... what is it?"

Maddox, without thinking about it, had reached out to brush her face with his fingertips. "You've got ice cream on your nose."

"Well," she said, leaning forward, "shouldn't you do something about that?"

He lightly kissed it off.

"Excuse me? Mr. Murphy?"

Maddox jerked away and grinned sheepishly at the elderly couple craning around from the next table over. It turned out they wanted to shake his hand for winning the election. After that, there was a steady stream of well-wishers, including nearly every person who came into the café.

"I kinda miss being a nobody," Maddox admitted during a lull. The waitress brought them fresh coffee, on the house. These days, they kept coffee at home, but he had to admit it ... he was starting to get used to tea.

"Oh, enjoy your ten minutes of fame," Verity said, leaning against his arm. "Pretty soon you'll be missing the days when all you had to do was sit around and eat free pie."

They went out to the parking lot, angling toward Maddox's new truck. He'd bought it with some of the money from the out-of-court settlement they'd reached with Ducker's company, with the help of Darius's lawyers. Some of the rest of the money was going toward repairs to Verity's shop, while the remainder had been put into a savings account for Bailey's college fund.

Maddox still felt a sense of unreality sometimes, that this was really his life. He had a home, and family, and neighbors who liked him and came over with cookies, and his mate who loved him, that he got to go to bed with every night.

Putting on a sheriff's badge wouldn't make up for everything he'd done wrong in his life. But he realized he was looking forward to it anyway.

People like him weren't supposed to have happy endings like this.

But sometimes they got them.

"Well, now what?" Verity asked. "It looks like we have an

evening all to ourselves. I have some tea orders to fill, but ..."
She smiled. "I think they can wait until later, if you have any
ideas for *other* ways we might fill the time."

"Actually," he said, "I do."

Not too long later, the truck was bumping over the ruts
in a rural road. Verity clung to her seat. "You know," she said,
"I'm not sure this is what I had in mind."

"Just wait a little bit. We're almost there."

He stopped the truck at a wide place and got out, then
gave Verity a hand down to the sand. The afternoon sun was
winter-cool, and Maddox handed Verity her jacket before
shrugging into his own. The fragrance of the desert rose up
to greet them.

"Where are we?" Verity asked, turning her head.

"Not too far out of town. I asked around town, if I wanted
to look around some old mines, what might be some that I
could look at. This is on Jim Doherty's land—you know, guy
that owns the gas station, but he said if we wanted to poke
around, it was fine with him."

They picked their way up a winding path to the old mine,
and he watched, entranced, as Verity explored the entrance
with her fingers, running her hands across the old timbers
and stopping to marvel at old initials carved into the wood.

Maddox sat on a weathered, broken-down wheelbarrow
and waited for her to find what he wanted her to find, while
the sun sank lower and the chilly wind coming down from
the mountains left him glad of his jacket and wishing he'd
brought gloves. It was still disconcerting to find that the
desert could be cold, but there was snow on the upper peaks
of the mountains now, and he was looking forward to seeing
what Verity had told him, that it occasionally snowed in
Silvermine on particularly cold days.

"Oh!" Verity exclaimed, and Maddox looked over with a
smile. She was just stepping back from the mine entrance,

ZOE CHANT

holding the little box she'd found wedged into a crack in the weathered wood. She turned it over in her hands, touching it all over, a small antique tin box that he'd picked up cheaply in an antique store in town.

"Maddox, look what I found!"

"Do you think there's anything in it?" he asked, rising with a grunt of effort as his hip took his weight.

"I don't know." She shook it and held it close to her ear. "It sounds like there's something rattling around in there."

"Open it and find out."

She had to feel her way around the box's catch before figuring out how to open it. Maddox was now in a frenzy of impatience. He had to shove his hands into his pockets to stop himself from reaching out to help her.

"Oh, how odd," she murmured, touching the inside of the box. "All that's in here is ... it feels like a bit of wire perhaps? Or, no ... some sort of ... ring ..."

He could see the moment when the penny dropped for her, and she turned her face towards him, her gray eyes wide and shocked. Maddox reached out and took her hands gently, and she didn't stop him as he took the ring from the box and slid it onto her finger.

"About time," he said. "Thought we were gonna be out here all night."

"Maddox." Her voice was barely above a whisper.

"Don't you start crying on me now, lady."

"I'm not," she murmured, her voice tremulous. When he started to pull his hands back, she grabbed them and squeezed. "Aren't you going to say it?"

"Will you marry me?"

"Yes," she breathed out, and stood on tiptoe and kissed him until he was breathless. "Yes. A thousand times, yes."

"It's like a whole new world that I was never interested in before," she said as they sat in the mine entrance on a blanket Maddox had brought up from the truck, passing a bottle of water back and forth. She kept touching the ring, caressing it. The sun was low and red on the horizon. "I knew there were all these old ruins around, but I guess I didn't think there was anything for me in them. I didn't think it would be fun for me. But ..."

"You do like it."

"I do," she said, grinning at him. In the ruddy light of the setting sun, loose strands of hair from her braid curled around her face. "I don't think I'd want to come up here alone, but Bailey's already said there's a ghost town not too far outside Silvermine that she'd love to take me to. And if you don't mind—I don't plan to drag you deep into any caves, but just maybe poking around a little ..."

"It sounds fun." And it did. As long as they didn't go deep; he still remembered the oppressive closeness of those pitch-black tunnels.

But darkness was Verity's entire world. In time, he thought he might learn to like it, too. She had never wanted to travel before meeting him, and now he was glorying in watching her world open up a little wider every day. It seemed only fair to meet her halfway, and share a little of her world with her.

For now, though ... "It's getting dark," he said, and Verity laughed. "Yeah, well, you don't have to drive in it. We'd better head back."

"Of course." She took his hand and he helped her up, then brushed the sand off the blanket and folded it under his arm. They walked back to the truck in the gathering dusk, Verity touching the ring on her finger every so often as if to be sure it was still there.

Men like him weren't supposed to get happy endings. But sometimes you could earn one.

If you enjoyed this book, please join my mailing list so you won't miss anything! ***Babysitter Bear***, Bodyguard Shifters #7, is out on Amazon now!
http://www.zoechant.com/join-my-mailing-list/

There is also a convenient boxed set of the first four books in the series.

A NOTE FROM ZOE CHANT

Thank you for buying my book! I hope you enjoyed it. If you'd like to be emailed when I release my next book, please click here to be added to my mailing list: http://www. zoechant.com/join-my-mailing-list/. You can also visit my webpage at zoechant.com or follow me on Facebook or Twitter. You are also invited to join my VIP Readers Group on Facebook!

Please consider reviewing *Bull in a Tea Shop*, even if you only write a line or two. I appreciate all reviews, whether positive or negative.

Cover art: © Depositphoto.com

ALSO BY ZOE CHANT

Stone Shifters

Stoneskin Dragon

Stonewing Guardian

Stoneheart Lion (forthcoming)

Bodyguard Shifters

Bearista

Pet Rescue Panther

Bear in a Bookshop

Day Care Dragon

Bull in a Tea Shop

Dancer Dragon

Babysitter Bear

There is a convenient boxed set of the first four books.

Bears of Pinerock County

Sheriff Bear

Bad Boy Bear

Alpha Rancher Bear

Mountain Guardian Bear

Hired Bear

A Pinerock Christmas

Boxed Set #1 (collects Books 1-3)

Boxed Set #2 (collects Books 4-6)

And more ... see my website for a full list at zoechant.com!

~

If you enjoyed this book, you might also like my paranormal
romance and sci-fi romance written as Lauren Esker!

Shifter Agents

Handcuffed to the Bear

Guard Wolf

Dragon's Luck

Tiger in the Hot Zone

Shifter Agents Boxed Set #1

(Collecting *Handcuffed to the Bear, Guard Wolf,* and *Dragon's Luck*)

Standalone Paranormal Romance

Wolf in Sheep's Clothing

Keeping Her Pride

Warriors of Galatea

Metal Wolf

Metal Dragon

Metal Pirate